Owen Meredith

The Ring of Amasis

Vol. I

SALZWASSER VERLAG

Owen Meredith

The Ring of Amasis

Vol. I

Reprint of the original, first published in 1863.

1st Edition 2022 | ISBN: 978-3-37500-269-5

Verlag (Publisher): Salzwasser Verlag GmbH, Zeilweg 44, 60439 Frankfurt, Deutschland
Vertretungsberechtigt (Authorized to represent): E. Roepke, Zeilweg 44, 60439 Frankfurt, Deutschland
Druck (Print): Books on Demand GmbH, In de Tarpen 42, 22848 Norderstedt, Deutschland

THE RING OF AMASIS.

VOLUME I.

THE
RING OF AMASIS.

FROM THE PAPERS OF A GERMAN PHYSICIAN.

EDITED BY

OWEN MEREDITH.

IN TWO VOLUMES.—Vol. I.

LONDON:

1863.

CONTENTS OF VOL. I.

PART I.

THE PHYSICIAN.

Polonius. This is too long.
Hamlet. It shall to the barber's with your beard.
Hamlet, act ii., scene 2.

BOOK I.

The Loreley.

Wherewith she sits on diamond rocks,
Sleeking her soft alluring locks.
MILTON—*Comus.*

BOOK II.

The Secret.

Mac. Canst thou not minister to a mind diseased;
Pluck from the memory a rooted sorrow;
Raze out the written troubles of the brain;
And with some sweet oblivious antidote
Cleanse the stuffed bosom of that perilous stuff
That weighs upon the heart?
Doct. Therein the patient
Must minister to himself.
Mac. Throw physic to the dogs. I'll none of it.—*Macbeth.*

CONTENTS OF VOL. I.

PART II.

THE PATIENT.

To tread a maze that never shall have end,
To burn in sighs and starve in daily tears,
To climb a hill, and never to descend,
Giants to kill, and quake at childish fears,
To pine for food, and watch th' Hesperian tree,
To thirst for drink, and nectar still to draw,
To live accurst, whom men hold blest to be,
And weep those wrongs which never creature saw.

HENRY CONSTABLE.

BOOK I.

A Seed from the Tomb.

The story of my life,
And the particular accidents gone by.

Tempest, act v.

INTRODUCTION

BY THE EDITOR.

WHEN my friend Dr. N—— assented (and that very reluctantly) to a request which perhaps involved some rashness on my part, that he would make known to the public the circumstances herein narrated, I felt that I could not refuse compliance with the condition affixed to this consent by the Doctor, viz., that I should translate and edit these papers for publication in England. I have done so to the best of my ability, and here is the result.

Although I must plead guilty to having occasionally exceeded the duty of a translator by some interpolations of my own which may perhaps be easily detected, yet, on the whole, I have been constrained to abandon the attempt to make such comprehensive alterations as I could have desired for the correction of what, on closer inspection, I must allow to be the defects of the work: for this I have found to be impossible without an entire relinquishment of the purpose of the original Author, as well as a complete transformation of his literary idiosyncracies.

It is indeed exclusively as the work of a German mind that the book can be fairly considered. This alone can account for the fantastic nature of its story both in conception and general treatment, as well as for a certain vague mysticism in the more metaphysical significations with which the Author interweaves the thread of his narrative. Whatever interest it may possess for an English reader, therefore, will probably be less in the conduct of the tale, or even in the examination of characters so exceptional as those introduced, than in such detached passages as indicate the peculiar fancy or sentiment of the writer. Yet even these I fear have lost, in my necessarily imperfect version of them, that occasional felicity of form and expression which, as evinced in their native German, induced me to undertake a task of which the result is now offered to the public with greater curiosity than confidence; and rather because, under the influence of many circumstances connected with my personal knowledge of the writer, my own sensations as a reader were in the first instance strongly excited, than because I have any reason to feel satisfied with my present attempt, as a translator, to convey to the minds of other readers the impressions thus made upon my own.

CORRIGENDA.

Vol. I. p. 41, line 17, *for* "Von Braven Mann" *read* "vom braven Mann."

" p. 87, line 3, *for* "Grande" *read* "Grand."

" p. 239, line 16, *for* "four" *read* "fourteen."

Vol. II. p. 49, line 11, *for* "Königlicher Preussischer" *read* "Köninglich Preussischer."

" p. 194, after line 10, *insert*, "'Now, Juliet, you cannot escape me!'"

PART I.

THE DOCTOR.

Polonius. This is too long.
Hamlet. It shall to the barber's with your beard.

Hamlet, act ii., scene 2.

from all she is, and all she must remain, upon the fretful nether earth, to all she would be, all she trusts to become, in the serene completion of some much-needed world beyond. This is no rhapsody. I feel and believe what I say; and I avow that it is with reluctance, almost with loathing, that I ever look up from the lowly barriers of the orchestra to those sumptuous boxes above it, where the same bloated cherubs eternally leer at each other across the same insipid arabesque. In those boxes sit the victims of the great world's great *ennui*. Fine ladies and gentlemen, who "come late," like Count Isolani in the play; but not like Isolani, who, at least, did not come with empty hands. These come, for the most part, with empty hearts and empty heads. What is Hecuba to them, or they to Hecuba? Far dearer to me, I confess, is that dingy orchestra, behind whose smoky lamps, among whose greasy pulpits, smudged and soiled with the long, long labour of how many an arduous rehearsal, I recognise the great workshop; the strong furnace, wherein the mighty forces of Music toil and toss, and seethe and heave, till glowing as with strenuous heat, the molten melodies of golden sound flow smooth into the sweet and stately mould of the Master's noble Thought.

How softly, one by one, and with what thoughtful faces, made melancholy by so much loving labour, enter, each to his nightly station behind his dusky music-desk, the gentle makers of sweet sounds! With what tender care the violin is lifted from its little case! Doubtless the poor fiddler's wife has no such snowy satin robe as that from which he fondly unfolds his cherished *Cre-*

monese. It must be an *Amati.* But, soft you! what is that wandering tone, pathetic and yet glad, like the sound of some old fable which we loved to hear when we were children? It is the horn. Thank heaven! the true *Waldhorn*—no new-fangled mechanical cornet-à-pistons. Now the sounds seem straining into unison. You half distinguish faint indications of a coming harmony. Now they fall asunder. All is discord and objurgation. The violin, upon its highest chord, is beginning to confide to the English horn strange news which it has just received under seal of strictest secresy from the clarionette. But the bass-viol, with four sharp fifths, breaks in imperative, interrupts the babblers, and severely calls them back to a sense of duty and responsibility. The drowsy double-bass, in lazy mood, as he leans against the wall, begins to clear his throat. The lugubrious bassoon gurgles twenty times over his one poor little part, making the most of himself, like an old opera-singer. The trumpet, not having to tune himself, is doing his best to put all his neighbours out of tune. But, softly, softly! There sits yonder, by those two brazen bowls, stretched over with dusky parchment, one who seems the master wizard of this wondrous sorcery. His brow is wrinkled into music-scores; his sunken eyes are like two hollow breves; his hair is white and thin. Softly, softly! he taps with muffled wand at the door of the unknown world. And now, sharp through the tuneless tumult, as with a will and a meaning of its own, strikes the shrill, clear, long-drawn, silvery note of the hautboy. Keen-edged and incisive the long note streams, like a sunbeam across the dark, through some chink of a broken wall. And as the dancing motes of golden dust rush into sudden revelation, and begin to waver softly up and down that slant, thin, shining track of light, so now the multitude of foolish notes, smitten by the shrill high note of the hautboy, forthwith enter into the strange significance of that sound, and assume a movement and a meaning not their own.

Reader, this digression is not idle. It closely concerns every incident of this history; throughout which, if you have a musical ear, you, who read, will recognise again and again, as I, who write, have been made to recognise it, that particular, unmistakeable note of the hautboy. Certainly the conversation to which I am about to refer, was to the full as senseless, and far more insipid, than the fitful sounds from my imaginary orchestra. But throughout every phase of it, constantly recurring, dominating all, giving to words insignificant and idle a singular and sinister significance, clear, cold, uncomfortable, premonitory of things to come, I distinctly distinguished that long sharp note of the hautboy.

For years, too, I have been haunted by the sound of it. For years I have heard it, after long intervals of forgetfulness, at moments when I least expected, and was least prepared, to hear it. I hear it now as my memory reverts to past events. Perhaps I shall continue to hear it till I have closed this narrative, which, by its restless recurrence, like an unlaid ghost, it has compelled me to commence.

In the present instance it was but a single word that thus impressed me—a word, too, so hackneyed and familiar, that I cannot account for the strangely unfamiliar sensation with which it affected me.

And what was that word, do you ask?

It was the name of the Loreley.

CHAPTER II.

The Loreley. Strange conduct of a Gentleman in Black.

THE two small cannons with which, soon after starting, we had saluted the Rheinstein, had long since been charged again, and we were now approaching the spot where they were to enable our little craft to do due honour to her mysterious godmother, the celebrated Loreley. The prospect of so soon passing the abode of that famous enchantress had probably led my fellow-travellers into a discussion of the peculiar character assigned to her by the various legends of which she is the heroine.

A sentimental young lady with a fat waxen face and flat flaxen hair, whose affected accent was of pure Berlin quality, had enthusiastically undertaken (no doubt in the conviction that she was thereby vindicating the cause of sentiment and sensibility) the defence of those anthropophagal tendencies attributed to that melodious Lady Witch; who, to the great detriment of the musical public of former times, is well known to have been in the habit of terminating her concerts by drowning her auditory. This romantic young lady expatiated with so much gusto upon the exquisite poetry and refinement of those very objectionable proceedings on the part of the Loreley, that we all felt persuaded, if she could have sat upon a rock and sung *Kuken** songs,

* A once popular composer of sentimental songs in Germany.

that the whole of the Prussian army would be forced to take swimming lessons. A slim sub-lieutenant, however, who was there on the way to his garrison at Cologne, appeared to be greatly scandalized by the thought of the disadvantageous and ungraceful position in which the lords of the creation would be placed when thus compelled to become the ungainly imitators of the four-handed frog. He vehemently objected to the conduct of the Loreley in former times. For his part, he avowed, he had no taste for that antiquated ballad-singer, whose behaviour had been simply abominable, and could only have been tolerated under a very imperfect state of the criminal code. Such things were, happily, now-a-days quite impossible. He could see in them nothing at all poetical; but much that infringed the police regulations. Any person capable of calmly contemplating the agonies of a drowning man was neither more nor less than a criminal of the worst description, who ought to be—not applauded, but hanged.

Here the conversation was suddenly interrupted by a loud clatter. We all turned round, startled and annoyed. Close to the last speaker, a table, before which had been seated a gentleman dressed in black, and of such unobtrusive appearance that, although everybody had seen, nobody had noticed him, was now violently overturned and thrown to the ground. It was impossible to suppose, however, that it had been upset by the stranger, who was at that moment walking away with such profound composure that he did not even appear to have noticed the noise which so much disturbed us. There was, moreover, an indescribable dignity and grace in the appearance and movement of this personage, which rendered it perfectly incredible that he should, under any circumstances, be capable of an awkward action. His countenance was of that kind which at once compels deference and inspires respect. The bearing and aspect of the whole man were what you would emphatically distinguish as unexceptionably *thoroughbred*. There was nothing in his features or his manners which repelled; but on looking at him you instinctively felt that it would be impossible to be familiar with him unless he graciously permitted you to be so. A vulgar or insolent fellow would not, you felt sure, be able to insult that man. As all that is vulgar and mean eludes and escapes the presence of an elevated and select nature so completely, that such a nature cannot even take cognizance of the existence of what is ignoble,—so I suppose there is in the perfect manners of the great, and the habitual consciousness of an unapproachably high social position, something which enables the few who possess it to pass through the crowd without ever coming into contact with it. This man was not only unapproachable; he was almost invisible. He was the image of plastic repose. Nothing about him was restless, or fidgety, or ill at ease. It was only by the indirect contrast of this extreme tranquillity both in dress and manner, that you unconsciously distinguished him from the ordinary mass of vulgar people who cannot ever sit still, or keep themselves quiet. His features were singularly faultless; but nobody would have ever thought of calling him a handsome man. You knew, but you did not notice that beauty of face. His countenance showed neither gaiety nor melancholy. It was smooth, and impassive as marble; and, indeed, so inexpressive, that even when you saw him you did not seem to see him. So that, as he now walked away from us, it was only by an effort of memory that we realized the fact of his having so long been present to our sight. Nobody spoke to him; nobody spoke of him; yet everybody must have observed him. For when he afterwards became the subject of our conversation, there appeared to have been a sort of tacit coincidence and agreement in our previous and separate observations; and we all called him "the Gentleman in Black."

He walked away from the capsized table so quietly and so unconcerned, that one of our party, in perfect astonishment at the inexplicable fall of that awkward piece of furniture, exclaimed to the waiter, who was busily restoring the sprawling thing to its legs, "Holloa! What is the meaning of this? Have you ghosts about here?"

The gentleman who made this inquiry would no doubt have been a believer in table-turning, if Mr. Home had emigrated to Europe in the year 1834.

"Well," said another who was sitting beside me, "if it was a ghost, I have seen him; and he was dressed in an infernally well-made suit of clothes, such as none but the devil's tailor knows the cut of."

"Ah!" cried the rest of the party all in a breath; "is it possible? The Gentleman in Black!"

To this explanation of the miracle I strongly objected. It was quite illogical, I asserted, and therefore, to me at least, impossible, to assume that the personage who had just left us was capable of an awkward, not to say an ill-bred, act. My ghost-seer, however, assured us all that he had distinctly seen the Gentleman in Black start up suddenly like a wooden figure pushed by a spring, and in so doing upset the table, just as the sub-lieutenant was laying down the law on cases of salvage. As on the strength of this positive testimony I found the majority entirely opposed to my theory of moral evidence, I soon relinquished the discussion, and withdrew from the debate.

CHAPTER III.

I DRAW MY OWN CONCLUSIONS ABOUT THE GENTLEMAN IN BLACK.

WE were now approaching the Loreley. I sauntered to the fore part of the vessel in order to secure a good view of that famous rock, once so fatal, now so innocent. As I passed by the funnel, I again noticed the mysterious stranger about whom we had all been talking. He was standing alone, close to the little step-ladder which had just been uncorded from the bulwarks, and was now slanted forward in readiness to be let down for any passengers that might be waiting at the next station. He stood erect with folded arms, and appeared to be contemplating the play of the violent water as it hissed, and seethed, and bubbled about the beating paddle. As I watched that calm and imperturbable eye fixed upon the boiling spray beneath, I could not help wondering how the passions could so completely desert the face of man, to lavish upon inanimate nature at least the semblance of intense emotion. The words of the Prussian sub-lieutenant rushed into my mind. In order to remain true to his nature, how should this man conduct himself, if a fellow-creature were drowning under his eyes? Would he shout for help? Would he exhort and stimulate others to the rescue, by shaking a purse full of sequins in their ears like the Count in Burger's ballad, *Von Braven Mann?* But how could he do this without instantaneously abdicating that prerogative of lofty and unassailable tranquillity which was proclaimed in every feature of his serene and severely beautiful countenance, in every outline of his self-composed and stately figure? It is told in an old story that a mortal was once admitted to the assembly of the gods. He was informed that, of the noble and majestic forms which he there beheld, one only was a man; and he was asked if he could recognize his fellow mortal. Amidst the true gods the one man, although he wore golden sandals and a purple fillet, and drank nectar with the rest of the Olympians, was at once detected by the *restlessness of his eyes.* Now as I silently studied the face of the man before me, I felt that if one line of those marble features were to change, the entire expression which commanded my admiration would fall at once like a mere mask, and be detected as a superficial grimace at the mercy of any rude chance that might choose to pluck it away. The soul wants not clothes; but if she once puts them on, they should so finely fit her, that she need never take them off.

Men with such faces as this should never change countenance, for fear they become contemptible. "No," I concluded; "that man must remain unmoved by the sight of a drowning creature."

The logic of this conclusion was irresistible; but I could not reconcile myself to accept it. I was glad when the cannons were discharged, and the explosion diverted my attention from the stranger.

The Loreley was not slow to return thanks for this salute. For my part, I even found her too garrulous. Any little real miracle would have pleased me better than that miraculously natural echo. No subtle song came winding from the wizard rock to enmesh the souls of men in the folly of a fatal bliss. Alas! No such songs are wanted now. The sorcery is fled from the earth; the folly remains.

CHAPTER IV.

UNFORESEEN OCCURRENCE AT SAINT GOAR. THE GENTLEMAN IN BLACK DISTINGUISHES HIMSELF.

THE bell sounded from St. Goar. The steamer slacked speed, and presently a little boat put out from the land. The only passengers it brought us were a woman and a child. The woman seemed to be of the middle class, and the child, a little boy, who was apparently asleep on her lap, might have been about six years old. Our captain shouted, "Ease her! Stop her!" from the paddle-box. The paddles stopped their play, and the vessel drifted leisurely with the stream. The vast waves that welled up from under her flanks, as if they were surprised at, and ashamed of, their own existence in that calm water, dashed off in a desperate hurry to reach the shore, and there hide themselves among the rushes. The little boat danced and rocked and dipped among these unnatural undulations.

My thoughts were still coquetting with the Lady Witch, when I was startled by a sharp and piercing scream from the water.

"Jesu Maria! my child, my child!"

At the same moment all the passengers rushed in violent agitation to that side of the vessel where I was standing by the step-ladder. I at once saw that the little boat had capsized; but how this had happened I could only guess.

It appeared that the boatman, in attempting

to catch the rope from the steamer, had lost his balance, and in the struggle of his fall had brought his clumsy and rickety little craft on her beam-ends. I saw him hauled up the sides of the vessel, while a sailor who had leaped from the ladder, succeeded in rescuing the poor woman just at the moment when she was being sucked under the paddle-wheel, and must, but for this timely rescue, have soon perished.

But the child? Where was the child? The steamer had drifted some way down with the current, and we could only see a long way off a small straw hat floating smoothly on the surface of the stream, with its bright blue ribbon fluttering in the wind.

After an instant of intense silence, however, there was a suppressed groan of anxiety from all on board. We could distinctly see the poor little fellow himself struggling desperately, and beating vainly with his tiny hands the headstrong water. His strength seemed to give way. He submerged, and we lost sight of him. No! now there is a loud cry from every soul on board: the little golden head reappears once more above the surface of the stream.

And now, again, there is a deep agonizing silence. Every eye is strained, every face is sharply stretched in one direction. For in that direction two dark arms of an audacious swimmer can now be seen, slowly cutting the waves.

Quite calmly, quite at his ease, with no haste, no precipitation, making each stroke with mathematical precision, as though he were swimming solely for his own pleasure, yet nevertheless with steady strength, as we all can see, leisurely gaining head against the sturdy current,—with perfect placidity and undisturbed self-composure,—slowly, methodically, onwards swims the dark swimmer. I must say there was something almost provoking in the extreme tranquillity, not to say indifference, of his movements; upon which we all felt that the life of a human being depended. And the singular and instantaneous accuracy with which the common sentiment of a crowd is always impressed upon the mind of each of its members, made me conscious that at that moment the swimmer was an object rather of indignant impatience than of grateful admiration. We all felt that he was not putting forth half the strength which he obviously possessed.

Now, now! he is within but a few arm-lengths of the sinking child. One last effort, one bold stroke, and the poor child is saved! No! Unconcerned, he has let the last desperate chance escape him. One stretch of that strong arm would have done it. One grasp of that firm hand might have easily seized the last patch of the blue blouse which has now sunk from our sight. Too late! The child has disappeared. There is a groan of angry sorrow from the crowd. But it cannot reach the swimmer. He too has disappeared from our gaze. My eyes are still fixed upon the spot where we last saw him. There is a silence of intolerable suspense. You can only hear the suppressed breathing of the crowd all round, and the careless sighing of the stream beneath.

That silence seemed as though it would last for ever; but after a few moments which felt like many ages, a loud shout of exultation bursts forth. Far, far away, from the spot on which all eyes were fixed; far away he rises again. *They* rise again. "Saved, thank God!" is the universal exclamation.

Now he is swimming back to the steamer —more leisurely even than before. He leans upon the current and lets it quietly bear him along with it. He is lazily pushing his rescued burthen before him as if it were a dead thing. He gives it only an occasional impulsion with his hand, whenever it seems to interfere with the comfort of his easy and convenient progress. And only an occasional convulsive movement in the limbs of the little body shows that life is not yet extinct. He seems to care nothing for the child he has saved, nothing for the intense interest of which he is himself the object. He appears utterly unconcerned.

And thus the Gentleman in Black regains the steamer.

All this passed rapidly under my eyes. The whole occurrence occupied only a few moments of time. They appeared an eternity. With that keen insight which belongs to strong emotion, I saw clearly into the inmost mind of all those who were around me at that moment. I recognised on every countenance my own agony; I detected in every eye my own thought. In all that crowd there was only one face on which I saw not the reflection of my own feelings; only one eye in which I could discover nothing akin to the sensations either of myself or my fellow-travellers. And suddenly, thrilled as I was, by the unutterable regard of that calm, cold, inexplicable eye, I again seemed to hear, with the same uncomfortable sensation, sharp and shrill, from some undistinguishable world of inner sounds, the long-drawn note of the hautboy.

CHAPTER V.

The Loreley in person.

YES! it was she. Angels and ministers of grace defend us! She—no dream, but fairer far than all that dreams can fashion—she herself, the Loreley! Beautiful, but with a chill and stony beauty, like the beauty of Medusa, that curdled the blood and froze the veins of men; calm, uncompassionate, pitiless, she was gazing (and I now knew she had long been gazing) upon this death-struggle for life, as though the agonies of it were to her the commonest matter of course, and the result of it a subject of supreme indifference. It had been sung to me in songs, I had read it in legends, I had dreamed it in dreams: I could not now mistake that gaze. It was the gaze of the Loreley. She sat as though she had nothing to do but to sleek her beautiful body in the sunshine, while her victims were gurgling their stifled death-cries in the dreadful gulfs far down. She sat, I say, high above the silly crowd; alone, upon the hood of the gangway near which I was standing; isolated, unnoticed, indifferent, even as the Lady Witch upon her rock. Her hidden arms drew tight across her bosom her long silken scarf, which, thus closely draped about her, left distinctly outlined the noble contour of her perfect shoulders. Now that I was suddenly made aware of her presence, I became, at the same moment, instinctively conscious that she had long been there, and that I had all this while been standing within the magic of that strange, cold, beautiful regard, and under the ghostlike gaze of that clear, spiritual eye. So indifferent to, and so abstracted from, the crowd around us,—so unlike to, and so dissociate from, all others,—did that strange woman appear, that in now beholding her I at once realized the conviction of how impossible it would have been for me to have noticed her presence, until (as in the case of the Gentleman in Black) some accident had forced my consciousness out of the limits of that trivial sphere within which those two apparitions must, I felt persuaded, in obedience to every law of their nature, remain invisible.

A new boat had now been sent out from the steamer; and the child, apparently lifeless, was picked up, and brought back to its mother. The strong swimmer, by whose exertions the little boy had been recovered, refused all assistance from the boat, and swam slowly after it towards the steamer. Nobody any longer paid the least attention to his proceedings. And, while the crowd on deck gathered with noisy but heartfelt congratulation round the poor mother, the saviour of her child entered the vessel unperceived.

I myself had not noticed his return. I remained spell-bound and immoveable under the melancholy eye of the Loreley; and I was still absorbed in the intense contemplation of the perplexing passionlessness of that Gorgonian face, when I suddenly perceived that he was standing before her.

But how changed were his features! Now for the first time I fully recognized all the noble beauty of them; for now those features were animated, for the first time since I had seen them, by an expression. And that expression was one of mute but passionate prayer. The whole countenance worked and laboured with the concentrated action of internal forces. The painful quivering of the lip, the deep imploring of the earnest eye,—all were agonizingly eloquent with the pathos of that unuttered appeal. And calmly, coldly, upon that imploring face, from the lofty heights of her chilly self-isolation, the beautiful Loreley looked down in silence, with the cruel dead tranquillity of her empty, unanswering, extinguished eye. Then, as with a supreme effort, from the long-labouring lip of the man before her, a voice, broken, and hollow, inarticulately muttered these words—"*Still never?*"

And sharp, freezing, and incisive, as the long shrill note of the hautboy, was the answer of the Loreley—"*Never!*" It sounded —(that short stern word, that meant so much, mocking the word it answered)—like a ghostly echo in a hollow, empty ruin, where nothing but such an echo any longer dwells.

For a moment the face of the man was swathed in a livid pallor as of death. The next moment those marble features had completely resumed their habitual repose; and he disappeared down the staircase into the cabin, noiseless, calmly, almost imperceptibly, as when some hours before, I had seen him leave the table just as it clattered down at my feet, and so greatly startled us all.

At that moment I was called away to attend to the child, and thus lost sight of the Loreley. This was my first actual practice as a physician. A glance at my little patient sufficed to assure me that only very simple restoratives were needed. And, having spoken a few words of encouragement and reassurance to the mother of the lad, I was turning away to give the necessary directions to the steward, when a grey-headed *valet-de-chambre*, the perfection of neat decorum, presented himself before us; and, bowing to the poor woman with that deference which is only manifested by the servants of persons of the highest breeding to those whom they assume to be of lower rank than their masters, respectfully requested the good woman, in the name of the Count and Countess R——, to do the Count and Countess the favour to join them in the private cabin, and to bring with her the little boy, for whose comfort and refreshment every preparation had been made.

Thus, I finally lost sight of the four human beings who were in any way associated in my mind with the mysterious side of that day's events; and, once more on the deck of the 'Loreley' steamer, the great Commonplace resumed "her ancient," but not "solitary reign."

CHAPTER VI.

PUBLIC OPINION. WE REACH COLOGNE. THE OLD CRANE ON THE OLD TOWER, AND WHAT IT SEEMS TO BE SAYING.

PUBLIC opinion on board the 'Loreley' steamer was much excited by the recent occurrence. Every body was asking "Who is the Gentleman in Black?" The steward, who was naturally our chief source of information on this subject, could tell us nothing more than that the name of the strange gentleman, whose conduct had excited such conflicting feelings and inspired so much curiosity amongst my fellow travellers, was Count Edmond R——; that he was the possessor of an immense *majorat* in Prussian Silesia, and the last descendant of a well-known and very ancient family.

The mysterious Loreley thus receded from the luminous realms of Fable, and only revealed herself to the common light of day as a Silesian countess! The stern and terrible sorceress, by whose spells I had been so magically mastered, was, by indisputable evidence, neither more nor less than the wife of Count Edmond R——. Others, however, besides myself, had noticed the extraordinary, and more than human, indifference which had characterized the conduct of the Witch, now reduced to the rank assigned to her by the *Almanac de Gotha.* She too, the wife of so noble a husband! a man of whom any woman (so we all averred) might well be proud! How had it been possible for that woman to watch with an eye so callous, and a countenance of such avowed and heartless unconcern, the noble conduct of the Count, when, at the imminent risk of his life he swam to the rescue of the drowning child? As you may well conceive, all the women vehemently condemned the Countess, and loudly extolled the Count.

In particular, the sentimental young lady of the waxen-flaxen charms, who, that morning, had so warmly defended the cause of the imaginary Loreley, and elaborately extolled the poetry and sublimity of the various misdeeds attributed to that duly-patented and well-established witch, was now emphatic, not to say hysterical, in the expression of her indignation at the heartless affectation of the Countess.

I may mention by the way, that this young

lady, at the moment of the recent catastrophe, had been duly careful not to let slip so favourable and appropriate an occasion for a little shrieking and fainting; which, on the whole, had been tolerably successful. The Prussian sub-lieutenant, for his part, declared that the Count had shown great incompetence, and was quite undeserving of the ignorant applause which had been lavished upon his supposed skill and coolness. He assured us that, but for the respect he paid to his uniform, and if he had not had straps to his trousers—(for indeed he might say, for the first time in his life, he had positively envied the gentleman on the Civil List)—he would have shown us all the proper way of saving a drowning person. That the child had been actually saved, was, he assured us, entirely due to the merest chance in the world; or rather, indeed, if the truth must be told, to his own perspicuity and energy; since he it was that had given express orders to send a boat to the swimmer, whereby the child had been taken up; though out of vanity, as everybody could see, the Count had refused for himself the proffered assistance. In all such cases it was absolutely necessary to follow a quite different method from that which had been adopted in the present instance. It was a mercy that the result had not been fatal. He had himself studied the true principles of natation at the Schwimm-Schule at Potsdam. For the practice of these principles, however, it was necessary to have a special costume, properly adapted for the purpose.

These views were opposed by a merchant from Hamburg; who observed that the chief danger to be apprehended in all attempts to rescue a drowning person, exists in the frantic efforts made by the drowning man to save himself; or in the involuntary cramps and convulsions which, so long as consciousness lasts, not unfrequently impede the efforts of the rescuing hand, and are known to have often proved fatal to both parties. The merit of the Count was in the calm and composure which he had had the presence of mind to preserve. Everybody could see that he might have hastened his speed, and that it would have been easy for him to have reached the child before it sank. But he rightly waited till the little limbs were exhausted; and so accurately calculated his distance, that the body must have reached him under the water in an exact line with the point at which he dived to secure it. This explanation was received as so satisfactory, that the Prussian sub-lieutenant, twisting his moustaches, growled out something about *Bürger Philister*, and stalked away with a loud clanking of spurs and sabre.

The Countess, however, was not without her defenders amongst the men; who, on the strength of the opinion offered by the Hamburg merchant, readily adopted the assumption that the Count was no doubt so admirable and experienced a swimmer, that his wife need have been under no reasonable apprehension for his safety.

At this point in the discussion, one of my fellow travellers, who till then had not joined in the conversation, informed us that some years ago he had had occasion to visit Heligoland; and that he had there heard the name of Count R—— frequently mentioned as that of a most intrepid and unrivalled swimmer. The feats attributed to the Count by the fishermen along that coast appeared indeed almost incredible. One of his exploits in particular was much talked of at the time.

One dark and tempestuous night a fishing-boat was wrecked within sight of land; and the alarm was given along the coast that all souls on board were in imminent danger. The boldest fisherman, however, did not dare to brave the breakers that night, and no man could be found who was willing in such a storm to expose his life to the hazard of an enterprise so absolutely desperate. Suddenly a mysterious stranger appeared amongst the terrified crowd. He said nothing, he betrayed no emotion, but everybody seemed to feel the presence of a superior will, and silently made way for him. He quietly picked up five of the great cables which had been hopelessly flung by, in the conviction of the impossibility of attempting a rescue. With the same composure and undisturbed precision, he firmly bound together with a small cord the ends of the five ropes; and taking the cord in his left hand, he silently plunged into the sea. In this way he succeeded in saving the five souls that were on board the sinking craft. That stranger was Count Edmond R——. And as, by a sort of instantaneous tacit instinct, we had all of us this morning given to the mysterious Count, the somewhat sinister title of "*the Gentleman in Black*," so the poor fisherfolk of Heligoland, ever after the event of that night, distinguished the heroic stranger by the more grateful appellation of "*Newfoundland.*"

Hence, no doubt, the indifference evinced by the Countess on the present occasion.

We all very cheerfully accepted this explanation of the lady's conduct, till to our no small astonishment, a certain very portly Königlich - Preussicher - Wirklicher - Geheimer-Ober-Bau-Rath declared that the whole of Silesia knew perfectly well that the Countess was touched in her mind.

This mental affection, he presumed, must be incurable, as he had never heard that any sort of treatment had been tried for it. The Count and Countess R—— lived in extreme seclusion all the year round at the Count's *majorat*, about ten miles from Breslau. They saw nobody; nobody ever saw them. There was no direct heir to the estate, which would lapse, at the death of the Count, to the collateral branch. And, therefore, nobody in

Silesia was at all concerned about their affairs.

This strange and unlooked-for announcement silenced all further conversation upon the subject. The little group of talkers soon afterwards broke up and dispersed, for we were approaching the end of our journey; and everybody, except myself, seemed satisfied to dismiss the matter from their minds.

What were precisely my own feelings as I walked musingly back to the bows of the boat, and leaned over the yellowing waters, it would be hard to say.

Deep under the death-white shroud of a profound and settled melancholy, which seemed to have permanently swathed in its cold and colourless beauty the faultless features of the Countess, my heart had detected the buried presence of an unutterable sorrow. One moment of luminous agony had revealed to me in the dark eye of the Count the torture of a soul, surely smitten by no earthly hand. "No," I said to myself. "Of the secret of these two souls, whatever that may be, I have at least seen enough to feel sure that it involves them both in the anguish of an *irreconciliable destiny.*"

The accident of the day, now nearly closed, had so long delayed the course of our little steamer, that the sunset was far spent when we passed slowly under the darkening walls of the old imperial city of Cologne. The evening was hushed and sleepy. Dreamlike we seemed to glide into the shadow of the ancient town. Above the deep and drowsy orange light that was now burning low down in the wasting west, rose, dark and calm into the airy twilight of the upper sky, the massive tower of the huge Cathedral. And high upon the summit of that tall, dark tower—high, and still, and solitary, as some old wizard on the watch—stood the giant crane, which is ever the first object to greet the eye of the traveller who enters Cologne.

Lonely and aloof under the darkening sky, it stood, with its long, gaunt arm stretched out, as though in wild appeal, towards the antique Dragon-stone; from whose venerable quarries had been hewn, age after age, and block by block, the vast pile on which it now stood—companionless between earth and heaven. To scale to the height of that supreme solitude had the heart of the Dragon rock been broken, and year by year his mighty limbs in massy morsels wrenched away. And now, alone under the melancholy stars, pillared upon piles of pillage, there stood the hoary robber, gazing sadly, as it seemed to me, at the wronged and ruined rock. As I lifted my eyes to that solitary image, so lifelike and so lonesome, with ever outstretched arm, and long-appealing gesture, seeming to look eternally in one direction, as though listening for an answer which will never come, I fancied that the old crane might be saying to the old rock: "Irrevocable is the Past, and sad and weary is the coming and the going of the endless years. And now, of the ancient time, are we two left alone upon the earth. Let us be reconciled to each other."

BOOK II.

The Secret.

Mac. Canst thou not minister to a mind diseased;
Pluck from the memory a rooted sorrow;
Raze out the written troubles of the brain;
And, with some sweet oblivious antidote,
Cleanse the stuffed bosom of that perilous stuff
That weighs upon the heart?
Doct. Therein the patient
Must minister to himself.
Mac. Throw physic to the dogs. I'll none of it.

Macbeth, act v., scene 4.

BOOK II.

CHAPTER I.

BIOGRAPHICAL AND PARENTHETICAL. CONTAINING SUNDRY REFLECTIONS UPON THE RELATIVE POSITION OF PHYSICIAN AND PATIENT.

AS events are to be told, *quorum pars fui*, it seems fitting that here, if anywhere, I should say something about myself. On this subject I have not much to say.

It was a justifiable custom of the old masters to paint their own portraits in the foreground of their pictures; nay, even to represent themselves therein as saints and apostles. Saints and apostles they were in their pictures, if not out of them; and this, no matter how well their tavern-doings may have been known to the pious public of their day.

But I have no such pretensions. Few men have hands strong or steady enough to hold up the mirror to their own nature, even in private. But to do this in public demands a courage which, happily, I am not called to evince; since I am writing only of others, *non tam sagax observator, quam simplex recitator*.

I lost my father when I was three years old. Perhaps the waters of the Beresina still roll over his unburied bones. My only knowledge of him was gathered from my mother's talk, and a miniature which represents him as a young cavalry captain in a French regiment.

In the year 1806 he was quartered with his garrison at B——, in Thuringia, where he made the acquaintance of my mother's family, and asked her hand in marriage. A stranger, a Frenchman, an enemy! You may conceive that my father's offer was civilly declined by the family. Still, the charm of my mother's beauty and goodness was such, that he could not reconcile himself to this refusal. In 1808 he was at Erfurt with the Emperor; obtained a short *congé;* revisited my mother's family; and so agreeably impressed them all by the cordiality of his manners, and the sincerity of his affection for my mother, that they could no longer refuse their consent; and the marriage was hastily concluded.

My mother accompanied her husband to France, where I was born, at St. Cloud, in 1809.

In 1812, my father's profession again called him to arms. On leaving my mother, he promised her that this campaign should be his last. He kept his word. Amidst the snows of the Beresina he perished.

My mother returned with the child to her own relations, and settled in Germany. She never married again, but devoted her widowhood to my education.

The first face to which my eyes were accustomed was a sad one. My mother's grief endeared to me the thought of a father whom I had never known. The story of his early death, and of the sufferings of those who perished amidst the frozen steppes in that disastrous retreat of the French army from Russia, I was soon familiar with. These stories made a profound impression upon my childish mind; to which I trace the passionate longing that impelled me, from my earliest years, to embrace a profession of which the object is to mitigate suffering and combat disease. This was my hobby even in the days when I was only able *equitare in arundine longo*—to ride a-cockhorse on a stick.

The face of my father on the miniature haunted my imagination in childhood. I seemed to see him perishing, neglected, upon the frozen banks of the Beresina; his dying eye turned on me, and his hand outstretched in vain appeal for help. I persuaded myself that his life might have been saved by the medical care and assistance which in those hideous solitudes it must have been impossible to obtain. My eyes ran over with tears; and when my mother said, "What is the matter with the child?" I flung myself into her arms, and said, "Dear mother, when I am a man, let me be a physician."

My mother was the only one of her family who encouraged in me this desire; which strengthened as I grew up. Her relations were scandalized to think that the member of a noble family should voluntarily become the member of a profession noble only in the beneficence of it. However, my own strong resolution, and my mother's gentle firmness, carried the point. A physician I became, and a physician I am; so far at least as the certificates of professors, some experience, and an ardent love of science can make me.

In the Faubourg St. Germain were still living some of my father's relations. This fact, but yet more the advanced state of medical science in France, decided me to begin my career as a physician in that country. I was on my way thither on the occasion that made me a witness to the events recorded in the preceding chapters.

Between me and those events there was now a space of two years; and between me and the Rhine, the mountain-chain of Les Vosges.

About this time I resolved to quit my modest chambers on the *Quai St. Michel.*

There, for two years, a very spider of science, I had hung my dingy web over the roofs of the most renowned hospitals in Europe, and dwelt, *tanquam in speculo positus*, ever ready to pounce upon each "interesting case," as the unsentimental language of medicine designates the most excruciated victims in the great torture-chamber of Disease. My time during these two years had not been wasted. I might now, if I pleased, return home with no meanly stored experience of the infinite domain of medical science. But I could not make up my mind to quit the most luxurious and refined capital in the world without having devoted some time and attention to what is called Society—in proportion as it is socially exclusive.

Some of my father's family still occupied

high positions, and were able to introduce me to those spheres of the Paris world which, ever since the days of the Grandé Monarque, have monopolised, almost without interruption, the despotic government of European taste and *bon ton.*

Know, therefore, O most dear and much revered Reader, that my address until further notice is, *Rue, et l'hôtel, de la Paix, au premier.* Wherein, moreover, *nota qua sedes fuerint*, replacing cases numberless of specimen bones, gleam cabinets of buhl, and porcelain vases. In lieu of lancets and Latin memoranda,—invitations, Opera tickets, and *billets-doux* strew my table and stuff my looking-glass. The hardly-earned title of "Doctor in Medicine," has disappeared from my visiting cards, and is replaced by a title due only to the accident of birth. I rise late, with the sun of Fashion. I lounge over the dainty breakfast of a delicate dandy. The lightest of phaetons, or the neatest of English hacks, takes me to the Champs Elysées and the Bois. Or else I saunter on the Boulevard, arm in arm with some one of the myriad friends—so lightly won, so lightly lost—wherewith that pleasant pavement is besprinkled ever. A dinner in the bow window at the Café de Paris, a stall at the Opera, and three or four *soirées* in the Faubourg, finish my day of strenuous inertness.

Whereat you shake your honoured heads, O my much disapproving, much respected friends!

Yet grant me a moment of your patience. I am *nunquam minus otiosus quam quum otiosus.*

In pleading my own cause, let me vindicate that of a profession dear to my heart.

The Doctor!

Dreary, living memorial, maintained by the sighs of humanity, in homage to the Fall of Man!

Doctors, undertakers, and hangmen, are beings whose presence society only puts up with because it cannot do without them. Nobody wishes to see much of them. Doctors! pah! ghouls! who remind us that we are nothing but a network of veins, muscles, and nervous fibre! Cynics of the dissecting room, whose eyes are sold to the contemplation of sickening things, whose minds are made up in the mould of a harsh materialism! Doctors! Nightmares of mankind, which endures them with a groan, only because each man, as an antidote to prejudice, carries in him a strong dose of superstition, and believes, when his body begins to plague him, that his dear life is in the hands of the leech.

So the Doctor is a despot after all, and rules by the fear of death. But society revenges itself. Despotism against despotism.

Let the Doctor dare only so much as lift his eyes, in the hope and love of a man's heart, on the daughter of the noble house, whose life he has just snatched from the opening grave with an energy and a skill unknown perhaps to science without love,—and frigidly you ask for his bill, and sublimely you ring the bell, and honestly you feel that rather to the arms of Death than to the arms of a Doctor, would you confide the rescued treasure!

I have much considered this.

In exaggeration itself the true measure can be found; since there it must be, otherwise how should it be exceeded?

Something of error I find on either side.

"There must be division of classes, and distinction between ranks," says the World. The World says well. He is a fool that would gainsay it: and whoever fights against Prejudice must expect to be worsted. For the odds are all to one. However hard this may appear, it is just.

I have seen in how cruel a dilemma those unhappy ones are placed, who, yielding to an impulse not otherwise than noble, have outraged the prejudice of class, and overleapt the barriers which it raised between two hearts. In the lives thus violently united I have detected an irremediable schism. And, even there, where shame and pride suppressed the groan of conscious failure, to my eyes, accustomed to trace them, a thousand symptoms have revealed the presence of the hidden worm, whose morose tooth, made more intolerable by the necessity of concealing the wound on which it worked, was gnawing disappointed hearts.

True,—I have also examined cases wherein all the world's exactest requirements had been obediently fulfilled; ay, even to the precise satisfaction of its highest pretension. Cases of failure wherein, nevertheless, rank, name, fortune, age, bodily and mental advantages, all reciprocities in short, were in unison to a degree that might sustain the quantitative analysis of Lavoisier. The temple was accurately built. But within the walls of it no Divinity abode.

Of all cases, these are the most puzzling.

One easily understands that disobedience to a law should entail unhappiness, if by obedience to the same law happiness is secured.

The Law of God, for instance, is entitled by all laws of logic to avenge the infraction of it. For fools may murmur as they will, but let any man loyally obey that law, and I will defy him to be unhappy.

But where this is not the case, where the strictest obedience to the law does not, as a necessary consequence, insure that happiness which disobedience forfeits, surely there must be "something rotten in the state of Denmark."

Let us not fear to say it: 'tis the law itself that is rotten.

In what? Perhaps in this:—

Cease to be *personages* only, and become *men*, if you will not forego the prerogatives of man. Cease to live by convention in the narrow pride of position, and begin to live naturally in the large pride of humanity, if you would enforce Nature's warrant to search life for human joy. But take heed,—do not deceive yourselves. If you are conscious that Nature is not in you, that *men* you are not, and never can become, then in God's name stick to your ranks and conventions, and thank Heaven that these, at least, enable you to be *something*.*

---

* Had my friend ever read the poems of Charles

All things are easier to us than to become fully and integrally that which we originally and naturally *are*. And if the dog-philosopher who, two thousand years ago, went about in the world, with lanthorn lighted at midday, to look for a *man*, were now again amongst us, perhaps he would no longer be at the pains even to search at all, but would blow out his lanthorn and keep contentedly kennelled in his tub.

"Vix sunt homines hoc nomine digni."

Churchill, he might have found in the following verses something like an anticipation of this thought:—

> "'Twas Nature's first intent
> Before their rank became their punishment,
> They should have pass'd for men, nor blush'd to prize
> The blessing she bestow'd," &c.
>
> CHURCHILL.—*Independence.*

But Diogenes was a cur. The noble mastiff is not to be roused by the snarling of a mongrel. To nothing less than man's sympathy for man, can man's worth reveal itself.

Between Christianity and Socialism there is all the difference in the world. Christianity says to the rich, Give. Socialism says to the poor, Take. A notable distinction! Let us seek, not to equalise, but to harmonise, ranks and classes.

"And who is better qualified to do this," I said to myself, "than the Physician? He whose subject and whose object are man?"

To find man in the Patient, by showing to the patient man in the Physician: this was my purpose.

Patient and Physician. Do not these represent the two most salient sides of humanity?

The sufferer: deserving love, because most needing love.

The healer, the restorer: deserving love, because most competent to love.

After all (may the ghost of Galen forgive me for saying it!) Medicine, if it be a science, is the science of guess-work and divination. The physician's business is to guess what nature needs. All that books can teach is to him no more than the flight of the birds, or the hue of the entrails to the augur; mere aids to intuition. Sympathy is the sole source of divination, for only sympathy can interpret the unknown. Sympathy is revelation.

Love one another, and help one another. You may write a thousand volumes upon ethics, but you will not add a jot to the divinity of this doctrine.

Well, this was the road that led me from the Quai St. Michel to the Rue de la Paix.

I say there are faults on both sides.

My duty, thenceforth, was to combat mutual prejudice.

The faults of the Physician, as a class, I knew. To emancipate myself from these, needed only a strong will, and strict adherence to a few simple principles deduced from personal experience. But from the faults of other classes to emancipate the patient? Of this I knew nothing, and felt that I never should know anything so long as I suffered myself to see in my patients nothing more than so many scientific "*subjects.*" Certain ills there are, which are only consequent to the manners and customs of a class.

How should the Physician cure these?

Submit to a medical regimen the many ways of living of the many classes of society?

You cannot do it.

Prevent young countesses from going to balls, prevent old gentlemen from drinking too much generous wine at sumptuous tables, prevent young gentlemen from passing their nights in playing at cards and drinking Champagne, by all means. If you can do this, Napoleon, by the side of you, was a tyro in the art of government.

But if the enemy is not to be banished by this or any other means, then let us study more narrowly his mode of warfare, that at least we may diminish his force, and resist his attacks.

The inferior classes are easy of access. They invite the approach of the observer.

The doors of poverty are off their hinges, and hang open.

Roofless and naked, misery crawls at your feet.

The middle class opens its hand to you with a welcome, and spontaneously lays bare to your friendly eye the process of its daily life. To this class the educated physician brings with him a fragrance of refinement which pleasantly refreshes an atmosphere close and clogged with the taint of the till and the storehouse. In the middle class the family doctor is the family friend.

Utilise to the utmost the advantage of your position, O my brothers in the healing art. You are the friends of mankind at large, for the foe you contend with is all men's enemy. Therefore you stand in singular relation to all classes. Mediate between them. The Divine Physician of humanity was content to call himself a Mediator. Mediate, also, ye. Three times an hour you are called from the straw pallet to the princely couch, from the pauper's hovel to the rich man's mansion. Here as there, in this as in that, pain meets your eye, and claims your care. For Disease, like Death, beats with equal foot on the thresholds of the rich and poor; and to you man's weakness opens the doors which are shut by his pride. Everywhere you have seen the equality of suffering. Everywhere you may mediate the equality of happiness.

But the doors of the great are guarded by an army of lacqueys. In the houses of the great it is only the sick room that opens to the physician. When the fear of death passes the door of that room, it strikes down the barrier which convalescence makes haste to rebuild. And if from time to time you meet again in the great world, the woman who, in her hour of supreme anxiety, flung out wild hands, and wailed to you for rescue, she will henceforth be to you only an apparition in which the arts of the toilet and the lessons of the dancing-master are combined to deceive your penetration, and lend to the body of disease the graceful semblance of a charm whose substantial virtue is only in the gift of health.

In that smiling vision of a pretty woman, bosomed in an airy cloud of palpitating gauze, with brows whereon the diamond lights defiance, and eyes that sparkle with the triumph of an hour, what shows you the cankerous thing that is gnawing at the core of the vital coil—gnawing at the core so fast, that haply from that brilliant apparition of the ball-room, to the wretched image on the bed of death, there is but a fainting fit, a syncope, a moment's giddy change?

I do protest it amazes me to have seen men whose names it is the pride of science to record,—men who, to the patient gasping in the agony of death, have predicted the day and hour of his recovery,—stamp their feet with angry impatience as they were leaving the door of some fine lady's boudoir, where, on costly cushions of the softest silk, the delicate *migraine* had spread its dainty couch.

O ye Samsons of science, whose strong hands have broken the jaws of young lions, and beat the baffled fever from his dearly-rescued prey,—witless as babies worried by a gnat have I seen you, unable quite, for all your pains, to stop the small, small noxious humming of that infinitesimal insect, commonly called *nerves*! Have I not heard you loudly denying its existence in the very moment when you were bullied, baffled, beaten, by the exasperating buzz of it? And then do you abuse the poor patient for not being able to emancipate herself from a morbid imagination. Emancipate *herself?* as if to be the emancipator were not specially *your* business, and this morbid imagination the very disease it behoves you to deal with!

"Don't drink strong tea; don't jade your nerves in crowded rooms; don't tire your strength in the night-long dance!"

Is that all you have to say to the sufferer?

But they do drink strong tea; they do go to crowded balls; they do dance from morning to night. They do nothing else, indeed.

Well, and what then?

Ether and sal volatile, and you are at the end of your pharmacopœia.

Bah!

Sympathising reader, do you now understand what induced me to seize the favouring chance that offered me admission into favoured circles? My object there was two-fold. I wished to rid myself by friction with the brilliant surface of that world, of the angularities of professional pedantry which the physician acquires from the habits of the dissecting-room and the hospital-ward; where he must harden his susceptibilities against the piteous moan and supplicating look, in order that his steady eye may miss no movement of the hand of the professor who is sawing the hipbone, or sewing the femoral artery of No. 73, and then hurry on to No. 87, without pausing by the bed where they have just thrown the death-sheet over No. 78.

I also wished to acquire and appropriate to my own uses, those fine tones and delicate touches of exterior culture, which are the art of the higher classes. For let it be fully acknowledged: the Great are artists; artists of the beautiful in common things, artists in the preservation of the graces of daily life. I am thankful to think that in human nature the tendency towards nobility is so ineradicable, that while, on the one hand, vulgarity itself is but a clumsy homage to something above,—on the other hand, even there, where nature is most artificial, Beauty receives its ultimate tribute in the perfected amenities of intercourse and purified forms of expression. For this, I faithfully respect those who, as a class, are faithful to the respect of themselves. Greatness is made up of little things greatly treated; and it is no small thing to realize in little matters the large sense of that lofty motto, "*Noblesse oblige.*"

With the result of my attempts to analyse the subtle perfume of that brilliant flower called High Life, in order that in the same corolla which contained the dainty poison I might find the delicate antidote, I have no reason to be dissatisfied. I acquired, indeed, —less by any scientific skill than by that tact which is the gift of daily experience—a reputation greater than my deserts.

But throughout this chronicle of fates not mine, I am resolved to speak no more about myself than what absolutely concerns my relation to the life of others. I am writing as it were under a spell; and the ghosts that have set this task upon me are already impatient, as I think. For again I seem to sit before the half-uplifted curtain of the drama of a dream. And again, as long ago, from far away into the hearing of my mind is borne, in warning or in menace, the phantom hautboy's melancholy note. By the side of thee, my Reader, I sit down, glad of thy safe human presence here, confronted as I am by these ghostly memories.

And now of thee also gladly would I know as much as of me thou now knowest, O my Reader.

CHAPTER II.

Apparitions.

IN this daily round of trivial circumstance my pleasantest hours were when, alone in the Bois de Boulogne, I let the reins lie idly on my horse's neck, and lazily indulged my own inclinations in suffering him to follow his. I speak of the old Bois de Boulogne, the Bois of many years ago, whose quiet groves were dear to solitude; not the new-made forest of to-day, which is chiefly dear to Fashion and the *Demi-monde*. Not more pleasant to my horse's feet was the soft thick-shaded sand along the thousand leafy alleys where he led me at his will and pleasure, than to my heart those many pastoral haunts so near to Paris, so far from the world, along the wooded banks of the Seine. Smiling Surène, or Mont Calvaire veiled in soberest autumn air. But chiefly I loved, and oftenest sought, that part of the wood, where, as you ride, at intervals behind the warm bird-haunted brakes you see in the pure, clear, evening light the gleaming of the quiet Mare d'Auteuil.

There, in true German fashion, I used to dream away the yellow ends of many an idle afternoon. For there, a weeping willow hangs over the glassy water, yearning to some mirrored image which it well knows how to hide. There the tall Italian poplars stand a-tiptoe, high above the comely trunks of good old oaks contentedly half-hidden in the mazy thicket underneath. But to those poplars comes the evening breeze with latest tidings of their own fair land. That is why they are so pensive all day long. The water itself feeds there, with constant cool, under the heavy summer heats, the green roots of a paradise of blooms. The iris, with his yellow cloven helm and sharp two-edged sword, steps boldly forward from the blossomy brinks. Like a little tree out of the crystal pool, upshoots, with graceful pyramid of white thick-clustered flowers, the delicate alisma. Midway along the liquid dark, float all day long at ease the large leaf-isles of the nymphæa. And there the restless water-spider weaves his swift-dissolving wizard circles round the dreamy, half-closed calyx of the lotus, leaning low.

Thither one evening, from the little village hard by where I put up my horse, I had strolled in time to see the setting sun of October twinkle through the airy webwork of the half-dismantled grove. I was sitting upon the roots of a hollow tree, and gazing at the west; where, though the sun was sunk, dark, bright-lipped clouds were dipping their moist mouths into a lingering liquid fire, to breathe it back in sombre light upon the shadowed land.

"Here," I said to myself, "so near the noisy metropolis of the world, is the very perfection of solitude!"

At that moment, across the profound calm of nature, I heard a voice of pain crying, "Cain! Cain!"

There was something in the suddenness

and the sound of that voice which made me shudder.

Startled, I looked all around me. I could see no human being. Every bird was silent in its nest. And still the voice cried, "Cain!"

Then silence.

From the grated greenery of the willow-tree not far off the voice had issued. But I sat still, stupefied and bewildered, without courage to approach that spot.

Again in accents of intensest pain the voice began to speak. Listening with a creepy awe, I heard it cry:—

"If thou wilt destroy me, dreadful Hand,—if thou art sworn to sink me to the abyss,—why then dost thou not pluck me by the hair, or seize me by the throat, and drag me down into the deeps from which thou risest thus?

If thou wilt have my heart, why dost thou not pierce this long-tormented breast with but a single sharply-daggered ray of thine intolerable amethyst? Be anything but what thou art. Rise rather on my path—not thus, cold Hand, not thus—but with fist firm-clenched, and arm of weightiest menace. Then will I grapple with thee hand to hand, ay, even till my bones be broken in thine iron grasp. But stretch not forth thus piteously to me those pale imploring fingers. Not thus! I cannot seize thee thus. Thou knowest it well. For fast the devilish amethyst has fixed me with his demon eye. And it burns, it burns —away!"

Then from the twilight shadows of the glimmering willow a man came forth, and instantly disappeared elsewhere into the dark and lonely woodland.

Instantly. Yet not so soon but what I had recognized his face. I had never forgotten that face. The man I had just seen, was the man I had seen two years before upon the deck of the 'Loreley.'

It was the Gentleman in Black.

I was strangely agitated by the unexpected and momentary reappearance of this man.

Night had long fallen, and all was dark around me, before I could rouse myself from the stupor of amazement into which I had been cast, no less by the mysterious and unintelligible words which I had overheard, than by the vivid recollections and undefined curiosity which those words had conjured back to my mind.

But at length I was conscious of a chilly change in the night air. I got up and walked back with bewildering sensations to the little village where I had left my horse.

My head was already in a whirl when I mounted and rode homewards. I rode fast, feeling that I was late, but hardly knowing how or where I rode.

A strong wind had risen, and violently swept forwards, up the road, twirling columns of fine white sand. I could see them plainly; for it was one of those nights in which the sky is darker than the earth, and the land was covered with a grey, melancholy glare. They moved sometimes beside me like spectres, as I galloped on, or—

"Lapland giants trotting by our side;"

—sometimes they rose erect before me, and

paused and hovered on the road as if in menace. To watch them whirling and changing shape as I galloped through them made me giddy. I felt my brain getting troubled, and my sight confused.

Suddenly on the summit of a tall, dark tree (as it seemed to me), I saw solemnly seated a strange, pale figure. It, too, I recognized at once. It was the figure of the woman I had seen two years before seated in the same attitude on the hatchway of the steamer. It was she herself, the Loreley!

Her dark mantle had slid from her cold white shoulder—cold and white as marble. Her long hair beat the wind. And a high, wild song of jubilee and lamentation—a song of deepest joy and deepest sorrow, she was chaunting or wailing in the plaintive murmur of the midnight storm. A song of subtlest sorcery it was; unearthly sweet, and wild with more than mortal pain; in meshes of a music magical, bewildering every headlong sense; and leading blindfold to the brinks of death the soul it thrilled with solemn shuddering and a deep delight. I felt the madness growing in me, as I gazed with charmed and spell-bound eyes upon the melancholy face of that alluring apparition.

Whilst I was yet looking at it, unconscious of all else, my horse shied, and sprang aside with a frightened bound. I lost my stirrup. The reins fell from my loose hand. Confused and afraid of falling, I tried to throw my arms round the neck of the horse.

Suddenly, as in a dream, I perceived that all the place was changed, and the things about me other than they were. The forest had disappeared, and given place all round to bare, black, pointed rocks, whose sharp peaks grazed with rugged edges the sullen sky. About the base of these black rocks fierce breakers, roaring, dashed their foamy surge, and tossed in air white mists of chilly spray.

That to which my arms were clinging fast was not my horse's neck, but the prow of a broken, sinking bark. That which I had taken for columns of white dust was a tumultuous crowd of desperate swimmers, shipwrecked like myself.

And we fiercely jostled each other, and fought and pushed, and struggled all together in the roaring gulf.

But high over all this, alone under the starless, dark night-sky, aloof upon her reach-less rock, sat cold the Loreley. And her calm intolerable eye was fixed upon that writhing knot of hideous human faces.

There, in the violent waters, all human passions seemed let loose. Desire and jealousy, and love and rage, and rapture and despair. And in every stormy face, the waves were tossing up and down, the passions of man contended more fiercely than the elements of nature in revolt. Each desperate swimmer was fiercely struggling to the savage rock where sat the Loreley. Each frenzied eye that glittered from the seething surge was fixed with hopeless passion on the face of the Sorceress.

And still she sat, and still she sang her solemn song, the cruel fair Enchantress!

But as, one by one, each fierce, impassioned

face was singled sharply out from the heaving human mass, and struck by the intense look of that cold eye that watched them from the rock, the face thus paralysed fell back, still staring to the last with glassy looks upon the Loreley, and dropped into the waves and disappeared. Each maddened swimmer, as that eye fell on him, flung up his arms, and was whirled away upon the roaring gulf, and seen no more.

And still she sat, and still she sang her solemn song; and still we helpless swimmers beat the boiling billows, and still the drowning men strove fiercely till they sunk.

At last I, too, felt myself suddenly touched by an icy ray from the eye of the Loreley.

Then towards her I stretched forth my arms, and cried :—

"O Loreley! dear Loreley! and I, too, suffer. But I believe in thee, dear Loreley. I do not think that thou desirest my destruction, though in thee I feel my fate. Speak to me, speak to me, O fair and far away! and tell me, tell me, that thou art she whom I have ever loved and must love evermore! Hear me, dear Loreley! speak to me, Loreley! say to me, say to me:—'Yes, I am she. I am Song. For I am the voice of your hearts, ye forlorn ones. But out of your hearts I am fled—long since, far away, and for ever. For in them I could not abide. For ever, for ever I have left ye, and ye seek me—for ever, for ever. And empty ye wander, and tuneless. Weary ye stray in the desert, and sad with your orphaned souls. And ever the poor soul is wringing her hands, and in vain. And ever she yearns, and ever she calls *Come back! Come back!* to the voice she remembers, and pines for, and mourns. The voice of your hearts that is fled. And ever without rest ye are urged to recapture that winged voice which from far, far off, makes moan.

"'But never that voice shall return to you; never, never shall you hear it save in the accents of an eternal longing eternally unfulfilled. Never shall the querulous chord that vibrates to the music of that voice find resolution; never shall the panging of your spirits be at rest. But in your pride ye perish. For never patient of the impossible; ever ye strive, and ever strive in vain, to overpass the bound that separates from your desire at its height, the height of a satisfaction which you contemplate in pain. And in the supreme moment of your desperate endeavour, when with wild hands and clamorous hearts you clamber at the summit, then with broken limbs you are hurled backward, and subside into the abyss.' . . . Tell me this, dear Loreley. Tell me that it is not thou who dost destroy us. And if I must never attain to thee, ever at least let me love thee, O thou fair and far away!"

I cried, I know not what; but words like these of passionate appeal. And tears, hot tears, were falling fast from those deep eyes, no longer cold or callous, of the Loreley.

They fell like soothing dews into the boiling, vaporous surge, and made sweet stillness on the violent waves. Then in that stillness, tenderest sounds of unimagined sweetness sunk softly down, and bathed with blissful music all my throbbing brow.

"Yes," the sweet sounds answered, "it is I. Thou hast known me. Thou hast divined my song. And the heavy curse which banished me, and bound me to the barren rock, is fallen away, and I come to thee, poor soul! I come."

Lower, lower from her lonely place, and nearer, nearer to me leaned the Loreley. Her white hand hovered over me in the hollow dark.

My own right hand, in ecstacy, I stretched, and seized * * * * *

CHAPTER III.

And what they leave behind them.

THIS was all I could recollect when, many days afterwards, I began slowly to recover from the effects of the violent shock I had received in falling from my horse.

A *fiacre*, returning empty from Auteuil to Paris on the evening referred to in the previous chapter, had found me lying senseless on the road. I must have fallen with violence against the trunk of a tree, for I had a severe contused wound on the forehead. And I suppose, from the torn state of my clothes, that, in falling, I may have caught my foot in the stirrup, and been dragged by my horse some yards along the road; for my hands were badly cut, and my coat completely in tatters. My visiting-cards, and the address on one or two letters which he found in my pocket-book, had enabled the cabman who picked me up, to bring me to my own house, where I remained insensible for many days.

The fantastic details, therefore, which, by an effort of memory, I have carefully put together in the preceding chapter, must have been only the images rapidly painted on the receding skirt of a dream (the hallucination of a giddy brain in a moment of delirium) by a consciousness already confused between fact and fancy. And the whole of my imaginary adventure with the Loreley, on which memory, in the mind's waking state, had impressed those proportions which are inherent to the habitual sense of time and space, must in reality have occupied only a few seconds.

I was convinced of this by a fact which enabled me to recall, with an accuracy that would otherwise, perhaps, have been impossible, the circumstances which preceded, and those which accompanied, my fall; and which proved that up to the moment when I first saw the apparition of the Loreley, I was in full possession of my senses.

On the evening when I was brought home senseless by the driver of the *fiacre*, my valet, in trying to get my clothes off me, found my right hand so firmly clenched together, that he had to force open the fingers. He then perceived that the hand was closed upon what it had doubtless been grasping when it was stiffened by the sort of tetanus produced by the violence of my fall—a piece of crumpled paper. As this paper was covered with writing which he could not understand, the valet surmised that it might possibly be of some importance; and, instead of destroying it, he put it aside, and placed it in my hands when I was sufficiently recovered, with the explanation here given.

I unfolded the paper carelessly enough, and glanced at it with indifference, convinced that it could contain nothing of the least interest; probably a prescription, or some old medical memoranda of no use to anybody; and I was just about to toss it aside with a sick man's usual impatience, when my eye was caught, and my interest instantly aroused, by these words written in German: "Fatal Hand, forbear! forbear! Why so heavily bruise a heart already broken?"

"This," I exclaimed, "can be no mere chance;" and with an ardour as great as my previous indifference, I began to read the manuscript. The characters were pale, and in many places quite effaced. The paper itself was so torn that the fragment was often quite unintelligible. I pieced the writing out, and put it together with extreme difficulty. So far as I could succeed in making anything out of it, it ran thus:—

"* * * [ch?]ase me, with never any rest, from land to land? Fatal Hand, forbear! forbear! Why so heavily bruise a heart already broken? Finish thy hateful work. I offer thee my throat. Throttle me, once for all, with those stiff fingers. I lay bare to thee my breast. Crush it! crush it! in thy giant grasp! Stifle here for evermore the painful breath of life; in its own cradle let it find its grave. And thou! thou whom * * * * more than a brother! Why must it needs have been thou, thou of all others who * * * * * the fatal ring * * * wicked chance * * * into thy hand? Had I not staked on it all my heart's felicity? all my soul's salvation? Did I not see in that moment the amethyst which Hell * * * * * * infernal flaming of those fires * * * * even then, when * * * * implore me * * *

* * * jealous demon * * * * too late! * * * * Everywhere under the water * * * * in vain! in vain! * * * * * brought senseless home? Then speech died on my lips. Then in search of death I wandered over the world. Was I not ever foremost in the ranks of those who were vowed to destruction by the wrath of the savage Tscherkess? Like the Roman of old who had heard, to his hurt, the voice of the augur, wrapped in the robe of despair, blindfold I rushed into the heart of the battle, invoking the gods to devote me 'to the dead, and to Mother Earth.' In vain! in vain! With a sigh of relief I saw the sword flash bare above me; with a sigh of relief I watched the muzzle of the gun levelled at my head

by the eye that never errs. What baulked them of a willing victim? What turned them from their certain aim, and my release?

"Ever, ever, the same! on the rocks of the Caucasus; amid the camps of the Circassian; in the howling Baltic billows; in the battle and the storm; that Hand! Why did I start like a stricken man, and fall to earth, when unawares I saw it on the stretched forefinger of a common signpost glittering at me? Then when, by my fall (thy work!) we were all saved from imminent sudden death under the tumbling rock? Ever thy ghostly hand, fearful protecting spectre! Enough! my punishment is greater than I can bear. What right hast thou to rob the grave? Let me die. * * * * * * *

Felix! Felix! * * * * that

should have blessed me, that has been my curse! And when the priest * * * * * * our union, did I not see in hers * * * * * * that froze the marrow of my bones? * * She herself, had she not seen it sparkle? And then * * * * * * * * * the frightful secret suppressed for years with the force of a giant, and endured with the fortitude of a martyr * * * * * * * in a moment of mad delirium! Ay, from the lips of fever the burning breath of hell streamed into her heart, and seared all pity in it, and hardened it for ever! * * * * * for ever! * * * * * * I saw her in the silent morning light, when all the world was still and holy,—I saw her

when, in the stillness, my heart was lifted up. Then when I began to bless God, thinking 'surely the bitterness of death is passed,' —I saw her by my bedside, watching,— another spectre! * * * * *
and her eyes were on me, and I could not answer her question."

Here the fragment ended. I could have no doubt that the writer of it was Count R——, and that, in some way or other, it had passed from his hands into mine. I had distinctly identified him with the solitary figure I had seen issuing from the willow-tree immediately after I had overheard those strange words which had so strongly affected my imagination, and between which and the contents of this page of manuscript, I could now trace an obvious connection. The Count may have been not far from me, somewhere in the forest at the time of my fall. This paper, which looked like the page of a private journal, he may have had with him at the time. Perhaps the wind had swept it away, perhaps he himself may have torn it out, crumpled it up, and tossed it from him, not deeming that the darkness of that night could have any eyes to read it. This paper, fluttering on the wind, and gleaming white in the night air, may have been the very thing which frightened my horse; the very thing which I had seized in my giddy trance, as I fell, supposing it to be the hand of the Loreley.

The events recorded in the first part of

this book, and which I witnessed on my way to Paris, had made upon me an impression hardly to be accounted for by the nature of the events themselves, which had in it nothing at all extraordinary. I had seen a boat upset, and a little boy rescued from drowning by a Silesian nobleman, who appeared to be a practised swimmer, — the husband of a woman of great beauty, with whom he did not seem to be very happily united. There was nothing wonderful in all this. Little boats will upset if they are carelessly managed; men who know how to swim will do what they can to save little boys from being drowned; and beautiful women will live on bad terms with their husbands, without any special exertions on the part of Fate.

But there are moments in life when, without any apparent preparation, some unseen Power lifts aside the veil which hides from our inward eye a world of things obscurely apprehended.

In the dead stagnant flats of daily life, when we have only a sleepy sense of being, and the leaden weight of accumulated triviality weighs us down, and keeps us low and lazy in the muddy bottom-bed of the running river of life, we are easily satisfied because our desires also are low and muddy—

"Rising to no fancy flies;"

—and we perceive not then the spiritual breeze that lightly ruffles the surface of the living element. But sometimes the deeps are disturbed, or sometimes we must come to the surface for air; and then we behold in a moment of time a world of strange, new things, bright and sharp and vivid, as they *really* are, and not flat and faint and hueless, as the smeared image of them is imperfectly reflected on the dull and heavy ooze of our customary perceptions.

There are undoubtedly moments of preternatural vision when the whole mind is in the eye, and achieves for our knowledge of the universe in man, what the telescope achieves for our knowledge of the universe outside. It annihilates time and space by calling the invisible into sight and bringing near what is distant. Lovers sometimes have this faculty of vision in moments of passion; poets in moments of genius. The former, in such moments, know each other's hearts at a glance; the latter, in such moments, know the whole world's heart at a glance.

Shakespeare, one might almost think, must have been in permanent possession of such a gift. When he, whose intuition seems superhuman, undertook to depict the birth of love, it is noteworthy that he did not select for the expression of it a single word from the inexhaustible treasures of his vast vocabulary.

In the thick of a thoughtless crowd two human beings meet each other. These two beings exchange a single momentary look; and all is consummated. Nothing has been said, and all is said. Nothing has been done, and all is done. The chain of fate snaps fast both ends of it, and shuts before,—behind. Every link in that chain of fatality is the logical sequence of a necessary law. We call it Love. And for the highest *earthly* expression of it, we know no other name than Romeo and Juliet.

It is worthy of notice how lovers are never tired of talking about eternity. With them everything, however common, assumes colossal proportions. They are to be satisfied with nothing less than For-ever. The vulgarest of men, who is probably incapable of loving anything for more than a few hours, does not scruple during those few hours to exercise a lover's established prerogative, and prate of eternity as though it were his to dispose of. Blame him not. He is sincere. What is the reason of this?

It is not hard to find. For what is Eternity but that which, being present, absorbs into its own presence, and so fully possesses, both past and future? Lovers do this when they love, even though their love may last but a moment. That moment *is* eternity. All that it contains belongs to eternity, and stands in vast and superlative proportions to the mean relations of time.

But such moments of intuition are not exclusively the property of lovers and men of genius.

It was in such a moment, years ago, on the deck of the 'Loreley,' that (I know not how) the entire fate of two hearts had been laid bare to my eye at a glance. And that so clearly, that I seemed to feel through and through their feelings, and look through and through their eyes, into the deepest depth of their being, without needing the knowledge of a single circumstance in their lives to guide me through the labyrinth of their lot. It was clear to me in that moment that what these two beings possessed in common was that which must eternally divide them from each other. A thought irreconcileable to union. I can find no other expression for what I mean; for what I mean is only vaguely expressed to my own apprehension.

But I was powerfully affected by what I saw and what I felt in that moment; and I am aware that it has impressed a special direction upon all my subsequent turn of thought and course of study.

From that moment all my studies were to me only in the sense of so many levers wherewith I was in hopes to force from its sockets the shut door, behind which are the mysterious chambers of the mind. It appeared to me that we doctors ought to bring all our endeavours to culminate on that point of being wherein the two-fold nature of man both falls together and falls asunder. It is not the body only, nor the mind only, which we have to consider as a thing by itself. Vainly we satiate fever with quinine if we cannot simultaneously provide the needful opiate for a worried brain. And vainly shall we administer morals to a mind diseased, if we cannot give support and energy to the will, by healing ministrations to the body. Hence the necessity of investigating the conditions of alliance between the different dynamics of life. *Alterius sic altera poscit opem.*

Extraordinary!

With this interjection we are apt to dismiss

from our minds those subjects to which we grudge even the most ordinary attention.

"Very remarkable," say we; thereby meaning that which 'twere waste of time either to mark or remark.

Yet it is by extraordinary revelations that ordinary facts become explicable. Madhouses and their inmates (not always perhaps so pitiable as in our world of sober sadness we esteem them) received my frequent visits. I followed with attention even the ravings of fever, but was specially studious of my own sensations.

Such studies, I confess, must necessarily remain imperfect, because therein the mind is simultaneously the subject and the instrument. To this I trace the comparatively small result hitherto attained by metaphysics.

I made my servant wake me frequently during the night, that I might, as it were, seize in the act the furtive process of my dreams, compare the influence of different hours, different conditions of body, and record my impressions while they were yet vivid.

These observations were destined to form materials for a psychological treatise, the completion of which I reserved for maturer years.

Thus, I had little difficulty in anatomising my recent hallucination in the Bois de Boulogne.

The events of more than two years ago, on board the steamer, had filled the background of my brain with a series of indistinct images or ideas. My second unexpected encounter with the Count had, by a sudden shock to the imaginative faculty, forced these images into the foreground of Fancy, thus approaching them nearer to reality. Realities themselves had simultaneously in the tumult of the elements assumed a fantastic character, thus approaching nearer to the action of the imagination.

The whole vision, with all its retinue of sights and sounds, had doubtless occupied but a few seconds in its passage over a brain already bewildered by the rush of blood, in which consciousness was at last extinguished. When I opened my notebook to record this new experience I found that my last entry was as follows.

CHAPTER IV.

Theory of Apparitions.

"Die Geisterwelt ist nicht verschlossen;
Dein Sinn ist zu, dein Herz ist todt."

"Unlock'd the world of spirits lies;
Thy sense is shut, thy heart is dead."

Goethe.—*Faust.*

SPECTRAL apparitions? phantoms? ghosts? visions?

Pooh! effects of imagination! nonsense!

Granted: for us, who do not experience them. But for the ghostseer, the visionary, what is proved by the fact that what *he* sees *I* do *not* see?

The verdict of the senses, negative to me, is affirmative to him. And if the thing imagined have no real existence, the imagination of it is not the less a reality. The proof of the *apparition* is that it *appears*.

What we call The Evidence of the Senses will, I think, if analysed, be found to consist of two distinct activities—Sensation and Inference.

Sensation alone cannot constitute the act of intelligent perception,—such, at least, as for all practical purposes we regard it.

For instance, we do not *see* the solidity of any object: we *infer* it. We do not *see* the cause of any sound: we *infer* it. Nay, we unconsciously infer the *images* of all objects from the nature of the action excited by the objects upon the nerves of sensation. For though the images of objects are reflected upon the retina, they cannot be reflected upon the brain; nor are they even reflected upon the retina in the position which is given to them by intelligent perception. Sight, therefore, is not an *image*, but a *sensation*. The *image* exists only in the *thought* produced by the sensation.

Hence, intelligent perception depends upon accuracy of inference rather than acuteness of sensation; and accuracy of inference must depend upon experience. It is so strong a tendency in our nature to project consciousness, as it were, by referring all sensation to external objects, that, if the act of inference (which completes what, for want of a better term, I must be content to call intelligent perception) were not constantly subordinated to judgment and experience, we should be led to ignore, or, at any rate, to misapprehend, that vast range of subjective sensations which constitutes so large a part of our consciousness.

There can be no doubt, however, that we are capable of seeing, and that very clearly, objects which have no immediate external counterpart, and hearing sounds, as well as tasting flavours, and smelling odours, which have no external cause. For instance, after looking at any object in a bright light, we shall continue, long after we have ceased to contemplate it, to see the same object, depicted in various colours upon a dark ground, or under the eyelid of a closed eye. And those cases are too common to be disputed in which sensation continues to be felt in limbs that have been amputated.

To me it is very doubtful whether such sensations can rightly be called imaginary. There is no physical proof that they are not actual, but rather the contrary; for it can be shown that in all such cases there is an actual excitation of the neurility of a nerve.

They can only be called imaginary when the act of *inference* which accompanies them excludes, or only partially accepts, the counter-evidence of other senses. This is the case in any strong cerebral excitement whenever the faculty of inference becomes deranged, and a single sensation is consequently suffered so to domineer over all others as to become hallucination:

Between hallucination, therefore, and intelligent perception, this would seem to be the practical difference: intelligent perception qualifies the assertion of each sensation by comparing it with the testimony of all others: in hallucination, this power of comparison has become either imperfect or impossible, so that purely subjective sensation is attributed to an *object* which only exists in the imagination. This is generally the case in sleep, where sensation is almost invariably subjective, yet never consciously so; dreams being only the efforts of the imagination or the understanding to account objectively for subjective sensation.

It has been ascertained that the image

even of an object in motion will remain on the retina, and continue to excite sensation in the nervous centre of the optic apparatus long after the object itself has been removed from the eye. And the sight of a horrible object will often haunt us for days, or weeks, or a yet longer time after the horrible object has ceased to be substantially before us. The duration of the spectre will in that case be probably proportioned to the horror occasioned by the object which has caused it, that is to say, to the shock upon the mind. But the shock upon the mind, if excessive or permanent, may react upon the body. A horrible sensation produces a horrible idea; the horrible idea reproduces a horrible sensation.

Here it is obvious that all physiological

inquiry touches very closely upon the domain of psychology. The practical physician cannot refuse his serious attention to that great region of all inquiry into the complicated nature of human consciousness. For there is a constant interchange between sensation and thought, between action and contemplation, between the outward and the inward, between objects and ideas, between mind and matter. This is the point to which I have wished to bring inquiry, or on which, at least, I would fix conjecture.

I dismiss from present consideration all those spectral phenomena of which the cause can be distinctly traced to conditions purely physical; such as the black dog of the Cardinal Crescentius and the like. These are nearly always amenable to medicaments and regimen.

For similar reasons I need not notice any of the current accounts of places supposed to be haunted. Whether these be old wives' fables or authenticated facts, they are equally removed from the scope of medical speculation, and have no interest for the present inquiry, which is solely concerned with the permanent relations between thought and sensation.

I assume a strong affection of the mind, either as cause or effect, in its relation to the action of a man. For example, of a criminal.

Let us suppose some passion to have taken possession of this man's mind.

That passion henceforward determines the course of his actions to the exclusion of all normal manifestations of the man's free will.

It becomes to him, so to speak, a *fatum* or destiny.

A human life obstructs the path of this passion. Passion marches straight to its object, and tolerates no obstacle by the way. Assassination has become a necessary step on the path prescribed to the man by the passion to which he has abdicated his will. The man avoids with horror the thought of this, which in turn, pursues, and never quits him till it has made him familiar with its presence. Occasion puts the knife into his hand. The victim falls.

From the series of criminal thoughts issues the criminal act; from the abstract, the concrete. The murderer awakes from his long dream of murder with the bloody knife in his hand.

The series of criminal thoughts belonged to the domain of one man's imagination; the bloody knife belongs to the domain of reality for all men.

Here the line is indicated which unites two points whereof each is stationed in a different world.

Let A be the ideal world, and B the real world.

A has conducted to B.

Therefore B conducts to A.

That is to say, reality conducts to imagination; action to vision. But as, in the parallelogram of forces, the action here is the resultant of the various activities contained in the imagination (*i. e.* the series of criminal thoughts) so the imagination, when acted on in turn, can take no other form than that which it has itself determined. And, either permanently or periodically, the murderer (supposing of course the case, as previously assumed, to be one of hallucination), renews the action in the vision; which shows him the bloody knife, and the victim's corpse, &c.

The vision exists for the actor, but for him *only*. Consequently, without preceding *action*, no permanent or periodical *vision* is possible. The series of criminal thoughts alone, without result of any kind in action (an A without a B) cannot produce permanent or periodical spectres. At least, I know of no such case. The blot upon the brain becomes palpable to the bodily eye only when the darkness of it has passed into the deed which stains a life.

The great poet of the English commonwealth says well:—

> "Evil into the mind of God or man
> May come and go, so unapproved, and leave
> No spot or blame behind." *

---

* Were it not (as the dates sufficiently establish) that the Doctor's speculations on this subject were written in the year 1836, I should certainly have surmised (notwithstanding a certain extravagance in his conclusions, to which a physiologist like Mr. Lewes would, no doubt, strongly demur) that he had previously read with attention that captivating work, "The Physiology of Common Life."

The dates, however, stubbornly forbid any supposition.—*Verbum Sap.*—The Editor.

CHAPTER V.

THEORY CONFOUNDED BY FACT.

IT is not without blushes that I now place on record this somewhat silly ebullition of the vanity of juvenile speculation. But at the time when I wrote the words just cited, the arrogant ardour of youth persuaded me that I had therein found safe foundation for a system of scientific thought. And yet, within a few weeks afterwards, half-a-dozen pencil-marks scrawled by a stranger's hand on a piece of crumpled paper, blown into my possession by the wind of accident, sufficed to place me in perplexity and mistrust before my barely-acquired conviction.

In that scrap of paper had I not before my eye proof positive that Count R—— was under the dreadful dominion of some periodical apparition independent of his will? But was it possible to believe that the noble and imposing countenance of the Count was simply a grimace assumed by a long-studied duplicity to mask the vulgar nature of a common criminal?

No, I could not do this. My whole mind indignantly revolted from such a suspicion. My theory, or this man's face?—which was the liar?

A fico for all the theories that ever were invented, if they theorise away man's wholesome faith in man!

But what then, in a soul so pure and lofty as that which seemed to reign royally at ease upon the open forehead of this strange being, could have occasioned effects so like the barking of a coward conscience at the memory of a crime?

Impossible to conceive! To me, at least, impossible.

Once more the life of this man seemed to thrust itself upon my own. And this time with an imperious pretension to enter into the inmost circle of those ideas, to the service of which I had dedicated my intelligence.

What had before allured me with the charm of a vague curiosity now impelled me with a command almost like that of a duty.

I felt bound to find again this mysterious

personage; to enter his inner life as he had entered mine; and to initiate myself into his secret with all the arrogated rights of a lawful claimant to an idea, who has been unjustly ousted from his due possession.

But my search was in vain.

I inquired at all the Embassies: I inquired of the police: I inquired at the public hotels, and the principal shops in Paris: and I utterly failed to find out anything about Count R——.

I was at last forced to give up all hope of tracing him. He had probably left Paris.

Besides, the day fixed for my own departure was near at hand; and my friends declared it to be absolutely incumbent on me not to quit the French capital without having duly visited all the wonders of it.

I am sorry and ashamed to say that I had not the moral courage to resist this stupid imposition, and my last days, therefore, were devoted to what is called "sight-seeing."

When I recall the days that are past, I am conscious of having submitted to so much needless discomfort and infructuous toil from a lazy inability to resist this sort of pretensions, that, bitterly lamenting the precious hours I have too often squandered in the payment of illegal imposts to unwarrantable prejudice, I am resolved for the future to prove myself a very Hampden in the matter of all such unjustifiable exactions. When I think of all I have suffered, and all that humanity is still suffering for the want of some Hampden-hearted man to vindicate the cause of individual freedom against this most odious of all direct taxes—the sight-seeing tax, which is a tax upon the eyes of a man, —*tumet jecur!* my gorge rises; and the spleen of my just indignation —— overflows into——

CHAPTER VI.

Advice to Sight-seers.

AFTER long stay in any place, in the moment when we are about to leave it, one thinks it a duty to see, in the most desperate hurry, everything in that place which one has had no care to see at one's leisure.

Monuments, museums, parks, public buildings, collections,—everything, from prisons to pagodas, puts on the obnoxious form of a tax-collector, and comes knocking at the doors of that respectable mansion, for which conscience already pays a sufficiently high rent to convention.

In that fretful, flurried, unsettling moment of man's fugitive life, when he is paying his bills and packing up his portmanteau, then is the time, of all others, when these importunate notorieties take mean advantage of his helpless condition, and vociferously insist on a visit. There is no appeasing them, but by submissive compliance with their demands; for they turn even our very friends into an army of touters.

And we call this—"seeing the curiosities of the place."

Yet I can conceive of no objects which a man should be less curious to see than those of which he knows beforehand that he will never see them again. O that "wallet" of Time, "wherein he puts alms for Oblivion!" O the things we stuff (and with what haste!) into that lumber-room of passing impressions, from which Memory can never afterwards fetch away a stick of serviceable furniture!

Animi fenestræ oculi. How do we fritter and dribble away this grand capital of sight! For sight is a capital, and it is not inexhaustible. How do we impoverish the exchequer of the eye by changing golden ingots into copper coins for the purchase of an infinite number of things of farthing value! How will ye rise in the retrospect of judgement against us, all ye lost looks and squandered glances! Poor, wasted pocket-money of that rich spendthrift, Want-of-thought! Thefts from the sacred heritage of Beauty maladministered by idle hours, untrustworthy guardians of a property not theirs!

O, dear Reader, if in the hour of thy departure from any place, thine eye hath yet left a look to spare, give it rather to thy neighbour's dog; for he at least, in some sort, will render thee the worth of it by a last friendly wag of his tail; but hang it not up, like a worn-out garment never to be used again, on the stony, callous cornice of some monument dedicated by the impatience of a moment to the importunity of Oblivion.

Is it not distressing to see men of a sober conduct, in the last moment of leaving a place where, for so many months or years, they have lived at ease and in dignity, suddenly plagued with this sight-seeing fever, "grin like a dog, and run to and fro in the city"?

If you ask them why they do this, they have no better answer than that "everybody does it."

What a frightful, invisible tyrant is this Everybody, who respects not the humble independence of Anybody!

Well, if thou canst, content thee with this Αὐτὸς ἔφα of the modern Pythagoreans. But as for me, *eheu! eheu!* what has it not cost me—what sweat! what toil!—in the going up and down of interminable stairs! whereby, *me Hercle!* I believe that I have exuded in the sweat of my brow many thousand shillingworths of knowledge, for which, may the generation of guides and door-keepers, if they be not condemned to hard labour at the stone of Sisyphus on my account, remember me favourably to their fellow Charons of a better world!

As for those modern Pythagoreans,—whenever by his *ipse dixit* I now detect one of them, I fear him as a man infected with a contagious disease. *Fœnum habet in cornu.* I take the alarm, and avoid that man by all means in my power, inwardly praying (since I would not be uncharitable) that it may graciously please Providence to remove him speedily from this world, and, if possible, take him to itself.

Mayst thou, also, O dear Reader, be ever able on all such occasions to exclaim "*Sic me servabit Apollo:*" and whenever thou shalt be pestered by these false prophets crying "Lo here!" and "Lo there!" may Heaven send thee grace to withstand them!

CHAPTER VII.

THE GAMBLING-HOUSE IN THE RUE ——.

THUS one evening, the programme arranged by some of my friends for the curiosity which they imputed to my sense of duty, happened to lead me to a place which I had never before visited, and which (I admit) merits one visit, but not two—to wit, a gambling-house.

It was one of those fashionable hells, which, at the time I am speaking of, were tolerated at Paris, and which, I am sorry to say, are to be found to-day in almost every German watering-place. The house in the Rue —— differed in no particular from the generality of those splendid temples of Fortune which assuredly need no description. But to me the scene I witnessed there was new, and, truth to say, it was not exactly what I had expected. To my thinking one essential element is wanting to the passion for play—namely, grandeur. Indeed, this feverish cupidity has nothing in common with passion except insatiability; and for this reason it does not seem to me to merit the noble name of passion.

Ambition, Love, nay even Inebriety, when it has not yet quite brutalised its victim, do in a certain sense, and to a certain extent, enlarge and exalt the faculties of those who yield to them; or else, at least, they force those faculties to produce themselves in some new and unusual form. With this it is otherwise. The player himself, indeed, may be violently agitated by the stupendous hazard of Fortune, which at one moment uplifts him on its topmost wave, and at another moment sinks him suddenly to the abyss. In the rapid alternation of triumph and despair, thus tossed to and fro between power and impuissance even to the point of insensibility, the mind of the gambler may perhaps present to him the image of himself as something Titanic and supermortal. But to the spectator he presents only the vile grimace of an assumed composure, which is neither natural nor admirable; or else the yet more painful image of a demoniac whose convulsion, under possession, can inspire no other feeling than repugnance.

I was already about to turn away disgusted, when the remarks exchanged amongst a crowd of spectators like myself, who had collected round the table for *Trente et Quarante*, attracted my attention, and induced me to join the group.

"'Pristie! He has put on Red for the fifteenth time, and won!"

I pushed my own with difficulty into the crowd of heads that were turned in the direction, where, on the opposite side of the table was seated the player, whose successful fidelity to a single colour had so greatly excited the admiration of the onlookers.

A heap of gold, piles of rouleaux and

notes, left me no doubt where to look for the favourite of Fortune.

Hardly could I repress a cry of astonishment on recognizing Count R——.

This time his appearance reminded me more vividly than ever of the scene on board the steamboat, when the coldness and fixity of his features, compared with the violent play of the boiling waters, had so strangely impressed me. For at this moment I could not but similarly contrast with the tumult of passions visible in the human waves that were fluctuating all round him, the same impassive, imperturbable quiescence on the face of that man.

The cards had just been shuffled for a new cut. Strongly impressed by a sense of the certainty with which the strange player seemed to carry fortune with him, the majority of the *Ponte* followed his example; and, as he did not yet seem willing to pocket his gains, new stakes covered that part of the table which, for the sixteenth time, had been so decisively favoured by luck.

Just at the moment, however, when the croupier cried, "*Le jeu est fait: rien ne va plus,*" the immense heap of gold and notes whose proprietor by his persistent adherence to Red had seduced all the other players to set their stakes on the same colour, was swiftly, almost imperceptibly, pushed across, on to the side of the contrary chance. Taken completely with surprise by this rapid movement, the other players let slip the decisive moment when, by following that movement, they also might have saved their money.

For, this time, Red lost; Black won.

The stranger, already so admired for his constant good luck, had by one of those instantaneous inspirations which are quite inexplicable, made Fortune his slave for the seventeenth time, and realised the highest sum which the bank remained in a condition to pay!

Everybody was astonished. I, myself, who had witnessed the whole operation, was at a loss to explain this instantaneous change of plan on the part of the player.

I had not for one moment taken my eyes off the Count. I was paralysed and confounded by the conflicting testimony of my own senses, which on the one hand affirmed that the stakes had been moved, and on the other hand that the player, whom I had been watching with intense attention, had never once stirred from the position in which he was sitting with folded arms, apparently quite unconcerned with the game.

It seemed impossible that he himself could have moved the stakes without my having noticed the action. But, if not he, who then could have moved them?

Everybody present must have been convinced that they were moved by the player himself. For nobody raised a single objection; and even the croupiers, who have the eyes of Argus, did not challenge the fairness and legality of the operation.

It is true that I was so occupied in watching the Count's face that I did not pay much attention to the table; and, though I am ready to swear that I did not see him move, I do not feel authorized to swear that I saw him *not* move. For certainly I saw the gold change places; and what must make me think that I was at that moment under the effect of a strongly excited imagination is the fact that, in the instant of transition from Red to Black, there seemed to me to flash out of the yellow heap, a quick, quivering ray of violet light, like the sparkle of a jewel rapidly moved.

But my impressions of that moment may well have been confused, for immediately all was in uproar and horror on every side. The croupiers started up, the players who had lost their last stake, and were hurrying angrily away, stopped short, and stared with alarmed faces at the Silesian.

His countenance had become overspread

with the pallor of death, and transfigured with terror. His eyes were starting from their sockets. His lips were blue and hideous. I saw his body, rigid as a corpse, sway heavily forward from the chair in which he was seated. The next moment he was stretched upon the floor insensible.

CHAPTER. VIII.

THE DOOR OF THE SECRET.

THE Count was carried unconscious into the adjoining room. I followed. When I mentioned that I was a physician, everybody made way for me. I was afraid of apoplexy, and judged it necessary to let blood immediately. I never go anywhere without my lancet-case. At my request the Count was placed upon a sofa. I bared his arm, applied the bandages, and made the necessary operation. When I had no further need of assistance everybody withdrew. I was left alone with my patient. All was silent.

At last, at last, I was at the door of the secret! Would it open to me?

For the first time, I was enabled to contemplate, unwitnessed, undisturbed, the tissue of noble lines which composed that beautiful proud face on which the semblance of death had now set its solemn seal.

Before me lay,—an open book, but hard to read, and writ in mystic characters,—the history of a profound sorrow.

"No!" I murmured; "impossible! Never can crime have established its loathsome workshop behind that pure, fair brow. In the musical harmony of those perfect features, I see no trace of that great discord —Vice."

The blood which I had let had relieved the head. The face of the Count, though still pale, had resumed a natural hue. The horror had left his countenance. He lay there calm as an infant asleep. His features had relapsed into that expression of noble repose which they seemed to owe to nature rather than to art.

"What Spirit of Reproach," I mused, "can have glided, furtive from the other world into this corporeal sphere, to execute in the soul of this man the office of the avenger?"

The more I examined the countenance on which I was gazing, the more did it inspire me with compassionate respect. There were lines upon the face which told of deep sorrow; but nothing mean, nothing vulgar.

"Vain," I muttered to myself, "vain, and

impuissant are the pity and commiseration of a feeble fellow-creature to arrest the retributive hand of Eternal Justice; but if it be only the toil of a too-sensitive self-scrutiny which has advanced thus perilously far that frontier which separates this visible material world from the realm of things unseen, then be thou sure, poor spirit, that there is one beside thee whose duty is to bring thee such aid as man may bring to man."

A deep sigh, and a feeble movement of the patient, announced the return of consciousness. I drew back softly. There was a profound silence which I did not dare to break.

After a short pause, the Count lifted up the arm which I had not bandaged, and motioned me to approach him. I obeyed. He took my hand in his, and looked long and wistfully into my face. Whatever was the object of this scrutiny he seemed satisfied by the result of it. A faint smile broke over his countenance, and without either false embarrassment or exaggerated cordiality, he addressed me in these words:—

"It is not for the first time, I think, that we now see each other; and I have a certain presentiment it will not be for the last time. I do not thank you. Towards you, indeed, the observance of an empty courtesy already appears to me too little; and yet more than this would, at present, seem to me too much. I wish you to do me the favour to accompany me home, in order that you may, if you think it necessary, complete those good offices which you have already so successfully commenced. I think I can now move without difficulty."

Silently, our hands clasped; and I left him, to order a *fiacre.*

In the next room I found the banker of the gambling-house, who, at my request, sent one of his servants to order a carriage from the nearest cabstand. I told the servant to wait for us with the carriage at the side door, where we would join him by the back staircase; and was about to return to the Count, when the banker stopped me.

"Pardon! One word, if you please, Monsieur le Docteur. The money?"

The door was half open, and the Count, who had heard this inquiry, rose before it was finished, and, joining us, answered it himself.

"I regret," said he, turning to the banker, "the discomfort which I have involuntarily caused you."

Then turning to me, "Monsieur—and your name?"

I gave it.

He bowed and resumed. "Monsieur de V—— will have the goodness to call upon you to-morrow, and dispose of half the money in accordance with my wishes; which he will allow me to communicate to him. The other half I request you to be good enough to distribute amongst the servants of your establishment, to whom I fear I have occasioned some trouble."

The carriage was announced, and I entered

it with the Count. We did not exchange a word on our way to his hotel, which was in the Faubourg St. Germain; a spacious apartment, *au premier*, which, with the exception of a few rare objects of art, had all the appearance of a house hired "ready furnished." The Count was evidently exhausted. His valet, who opened the door to us, and in whom I recognised the old servant I had before seen on board the steamer, did not speak a word of French. I explained to him in German that his master had had a slight accident, and gave him the few orders which I considered necessary for the night. The old man shook his head mournfully, and muttered several times—"Again, dear God! again? The Lord help us!"

I enjoined upon the Count the most perfect repose. A stupid counsel, which he received with an ironic smile, and of which I myself felt the utter futility.

"Pray do me the favour," he said, as we shook hands, "to let me see you again to-morrow."

I promised to call upon him the next day; and we parted for that night.

"I wonder," I said to myself, as I left the house, "whether I shall see again that woman's face."

CHAPTER IX.

Remains Shut.

THE next day I waited on Count Edmond R——, at the hour which I had been impatiently expecting. As I approached the house, I looked eagerly at the windows. No face at those windows; no Loreley there with beckoning hand. The blinds were drawn. Whatever sorrow inhabited those chambers had no voice. My heart was listening, but I heard not the note of the hautboy.

I was shown into a large saloon overlooking the court. Not a flower in the windows; not a broidery frame in the corner; not the ghost of a passing perfume; no bonnet, glove, or shawl upon the chair; no careless piece of needlework upon the table; no single gracious trace of a woman's presence, beautified the cheerless aspect of that hideous, formal furniture, which remains a monument to the bad taste of the "Great Empire."

Was she in this house? was she in Paris? or was the Count here quite alone?

I had not much time to look about me before Count R—— entered the room. Holding out both his hands, he came forward to meet me with gracious cordiality. All trace of the previous night's excitement had completely disappeared from his face and manner. It needed all that perspicuity which is only possessed by the practised eye of the physician to enable me to detect under this well-assumed mask of easy indifference, the struggle maintained by the power of a strong will against the effort of nature.

"You see in me," said the Count, smiling, "a flattering testimonial to your skill and experience. Your excellent treatment has done wonders; and I owe to your successful care a calm night and refreshing sleep: the greatest blessings which the craft of science can filch from the thrift of nature. Be seated. I feel stronger and better than ever. In this you have done me a double service. For the fact is, that pressing affairs, which compelled me to fix my departure for to-day, would have seriously suffered had I been obliged to postpone my return to Silesia. To-day, however, I feel so well, that, knowing by experience the strength of my constitution, I have no reason to fear the effects of a journey. Instead of thanks, permit me, rather, to increase my debt to you by a request."

This manœuvre, by which the Count obviously intended to prevent a closer approach upon my part, did not find me altogether unprepared. Before rejoining him that morning, I had reflected on what should be my line of conduct towards him, and what might possibly be the character of his towards me. I was resolved not to injure by any ill-timed or exaggerated advances the favourable impression on which chance (if chance it were?) had enabled me to found the hope of future intimacy; and I felt persuaded that a man, educated in all those refinements of life which render men's nature especially sensitive to the graces of little things, would instinctively shrink from the embrace of a clumsy cordiality.

Without betraying the least surprise or embarrassment, therefore, I immediately gave my consent to this proposal, which I could see to have been carefully prepared.

I could at once congratulate myself on the effect of my reply. For Count Edmond was not so completely master of his feelings (or did not care perhaps so completely to conceal them), but what I could seize, as it were, upon the wing, an expression of relief and satisfaction which flitted over his features.

"How enchanted I am," said he, "that we two, strangers as we are, so well understand each other!"

He cordially shook me by the hand, and I asked him for his last orders.

"No, no!" he replied, with a frank and pleasant smile, "not *last*, my dear sir. There is no such thing as last. At least I don't think that either you or I have much belief in that word. However, if you will have it so, this is my last *request*. You heard me, last night, dispose of your good offices without even awaiting your permission, by informing the banker at ——'s that you would be kind enough to call upon him in my name for a sum of money, which I am ashamed of having acquired in such a way, and of which the possession would be most repugnant to all my feelings. Indeed, I can assure you that I am no gambler. Curiosity led me (perhaps like yourself) to that house. I wished to pay my entrance by a small stake, and I only left my money upon the table for the purpose of getting rid of it. The rest you know."

He paused. His lip quivered for a moment, but he quickly resumed:—

"In telling me your name you recalled to my mind various associations which had hitherto attached themselves *only* to your name; for till then my good fortune had not favoured me with the pleasure of your personal acquaintance. Your name, however, had often been mentioned to me by friends of your mother's family, with whom I am slightly acquainted. I know the noble object of your life, and I have even been sometimes disposed to envy you the rewards of an existence so devoted to the welfare of others.

"Well, now, you see, I am going to intrude my participation upon this good work of yours. Favour me by accepting this small sum and applying it to the relief of that poverty and suffering, to the cause of which you have so generously dedicated your endeavours; and which, indeed, without your skill and sympathy, this slight offering of mine would be powerless to alleviate. And hereafter—"

I was going to speak, but he interrupted me, and went on rapidly:—

"Hereafter, whenever you fall in with

such cases of need as you may consider deserving, pray do not fail to regard me as your banker. Two lines from you to L——, near Breslau, with the address of the sufferer, will enable you to make at least *one* person happy, if not two. And now, adieu! We shall meet again. I feel it, without stopping at this moment to consider how, or where."

He shook me once more by the hand, and thus we took leave of each other.

Once more this strange figure receded from my sight into unknown distance: and the solution of the enigma on which I had thought to touch, slipped from my grasp, and left me as ignorant as I had been before.

This time, however, I felt that a sort of

link had been established between myself and this man. A link which time and distance might perhaps attenuate, but could not wholly dissolve.

CHAPTER X.

Home!

I EXECUTED with great satisfaction the last orders of Count R——. I only knew too well what to do with the money. Within my experience of this brilliant holiday Paris, there was no lack of tears to dry, nor of misery to mitigate. My own affairs did not detain me much longer in this town, which I was already impatient to leave. Nothing is more fatiguing than the days and weeks which precede an anticipated and inevitable departure.

I hailed with joy the hour which found me, on the stroke of six in the afternoon, before the great courtyard in the Rue Jean Jacques Rousseau.

Oh, happy days of most unvalued quiet, too rashly and too cheaply sold to the army of railway-contractors in exchange for sixty miles an hour, and spine diseases! Days, when life enjoyed the dignity of delay, when the world travelled by post, and the world's wife on a pillion! Then, as we jogged along the highway, I do verily believe that (in despite of Danton's ghost), high and low, rich and poor, wise and foolish, stood far enough asunder to be able to take a good look at each other as they passed along; and, as one says, "knew their places." Now, the journey of life is more rapid, but I'll be shot if I think it half so pleasant. For in the hurry-skurry we are so tumbled together, that who can say where he is, or where he will be? and 'tis but a sorry chance which of us may fall uppermost.

Six!—It clashes clear from the great dial; and the frosty twilight is falling.

Six!—And cheerily issues the first britska from the inner court, where these ponderous locomotives of an unlocomotive age used to lurk harnessed and ready when the hour struck to disperse themselves leisurely to the four quarters of the compass.

Bordeaux! shouts the *employé de la poste.* A couple of travellers jump into the carriage. The door shuts with a sharp click. The postilion blithely clacks his long-lashed, short-handled whip, and four colossal *percherons* strain forward in the traces, and start off at a brisk trot to the merry sound of a multitude of little tinkling bells.

Calais! Lyons! A second *calèche*: a third.

The *courrier* swings himself into the *cabriolet*. They are off.

At last, Strasbourg! How my heart beats! *O dulce germen matris!* (may the souls of the grammarians forgive me the pun!) O dear mother German! Home! and with what homeward thoughts I scale the high carriage step. We issue on to the great open spaces of the night, by the Barrier St. Denis. I plunge my yearning looks, beyond me, deep and far into the glimmering air; searching on the utmost verge of the dark horizon that long line of clouds, which may perhaps o'ercanopy (O pleasant thought!) the skies of Germany. And as the restless roar of Paris (that never quiet heart) sinks faint behind me on the serious, cold night air, I have little care to remember that I am leaving, perhaps for ever, a world, bottomless, vast; a world of vice and grandeur; of the ludicrous and the sublime.

PART II.

THE PATIENT.

To tread a maze that never shall have end,
To burn in sighs and starve in daily tears,
To climb a hill, and never to descend,
Giants to kill, and quake at childish fears,
To pine for food, and watch th' Hesperian tree,
To thirst for drink, and nectar still to draw,
To live accurst, whom men hold blest to be,
And weep those wrongs which never creature saw.

HENRY CONSTABLE.

BOOK I.

A Seed from the Tomb.

The story of my life
And the particular accidents gone by.

Tempest, act v.

BOOK I.

CHAPTER I.

St. Sylvester's Eve.

ANNO DOMINI, Eighteen Hundred and Forty-two.

In the heart of Silesia; in the good town of Breslau; anybody you may meet in the streets there will be able to show you the way to the Doctor's house; and if you care to see again an old acquaintance, come here. Come, winter or summer, when you will, sure of welcome. The guest-chamber is ever ready. You shall have the best room in the house; not without a gust of apple-blossoms at the window, if you come when the swallows are here; nor a merry twitter of redbreasts (old accustomed guests of mine) if you wait for the snow and frost. The best room in the house, did I say? nay, but you shall have the two best rooms in the house, if you will bring your wife with you. For since we parted at Paris, O very dear Reader, I, at least, am no longer a bachelor. My life is quieted and completed by the peaceful presence of a wise, kind woman-face; a face that makes itself more felt than seen. And there are little chirping voices about the rooms here. So, then, if you also bring with you any of that pleasant, provoking, noisy, busy little baggage, so much the better.

We will shut it all up in the nursery; where all day long it is full of the most important business, jumping and skipping up and down, and sliding about with sprawling foot and hand, and building palaces with chairs and cushions, and driving coaches, and blowing trumpets, and making to itself a hundred Iliads. For this is the Heroic Age.

Only, in truth, I would not have had you choose for the date of your visit that wild night of St. Sylvester, when this year of our Lord Eighteen Hundred and Forty-two was knocking, in snow and storm, at the creaking doors of Time. Sharply and bitterly, —not in welcome, not in love,—the Old Year, in his dying hour, snorted with icy breath in the face of his young usurper. Well may he have been muttering from his chappy lip,

"Turn back! turn back, ill-omened Brother! Set not thy fatal foot upon this poor distracted planet! For in thy dry and shining eyes I see the glare of fire and of famine. Thy hands are empty of the tilth, and the tithe thou hast consecrated to Death!"

But the New Year turned not back.

It turned not back before the gates of Hamburg; where the blithe bells rang with unsuspicious peals its treacherous entry into that devoted town. Bells soon made to ring far other music, when the midnight was bright with the glare, and hot with the breath, of the Destroying Angel. For then, swung fiercely by the unseen hands of the Spirits of Fire, they rang their own death knell; rang, till from their pious habitations and pure lives of gentle motion and sweet sound, they dropped, deformed dumb things; rang, till the burning metal trickled and crawled like boiling blood among their ruined homes, and became again dead earthy ore in earth.*

The New Year turned not back. It turned not back before the snow-capped forest-hills of Bohemia; whose greenest saplings had but lately shed such merry lustre in cottage and in palace, decked by young hands, to celebrate the blessed Christmas-time. Less merry a light was yours, old father pines, that rested in the forest! For nine days long the smoke of your burning overshadowed two kingdoms, and for nine nights long the

---

* One of the strangest phenomena of the great fire of Hamburg was the seemingly-spontaneous ringing of the bells, occasioned by the disturbance of the heated air,

glare of your fires made pale the stars of heaven, while the timid deer sought willingly the hunter's door.

It turned not back, that stern New Year, before many a threshold which Death had marked for sorrow. My own it passed with mourning, and a mother's loss.

Long, here in German land shall we remember thee, not lovingly, ill-fated year! Ay! till bells on Hamburg towers rebuilt ring in some better time: ay! till the ashes of those burnt forests pass again to living green: ah me! till Death with other kinder touchings has stopped the bleeding wounds in hearts which thou hast stricken.

Not upon this Sylvester's night, then, would I have had thee come, dear Reader, to test my hospitality. Not here, indeed, wouldst thou have found me; but by the lonely sick-bed of a dying man: not amidst merry little faces keeping holiday, but with prayer and supplication (the only medicine poured for him), keeping watch beside a long-outwearied spirit, whose sole physician was a friend. For there, upon that bed under which already the grave was yawning, lay stretched (much needing rest) the tired frame of Edmond Count R——.

CHAPTER II.

An Unexpected Visitor.

AFTER leaving Paris, I temporarily established myself in Berlin—a place of residence which I selected for the ready access it afforded me to those great reservoirs of physical suffering called hospitals, as well as for the intellectual atmosphere for which the Prussian capital is renowned. Not long, however, after I had pitched my tent amidst the Brandenburg sands, I received, and accepted, an invitation from Breslau to take the chair of the medical professorship at that university. Here I was fortunate enough to succeed in soon securing a connection which assured to me an easy, if not a brilliant, future.

Amongst the writings by which, immediately after my return from Paris, I had sought to introduce myself to the literary world in Germany, was a small pamphlet, intitled :—

A TREATISE
UPON
SPECTRAL APPARITIONS,
BEING
A CONTRIBUTION
TO THE
PHENOMENOLOGY OF THE BRAIN.

It fell still-born, however, and nearly

ruined my publishers, who were not men of capital.* Those of the τὶ νέον; class, who sought to stimulate a jaded imagination by new incredibilities, found the book flat and insipid: those, on the other hand, who were the constituted guardians of a languid experience, denounced it as flighty and fantastic. Thus the work failed to conciliate any portion of the public; and I myself, amidst the occupations of a daily-increasing practice, had almost entirely forgotten this early failure of my literary efforts, when it was suddenly recalled to my recollection by the event which I am about to relate.

---

* I hope, both for my own sake, and that of the highly-respected Firm who have undertaken the protection of it, that the Doctor's present invasion of the literary world may be less illfated.—EDITOR.

One night, I had returned home later than usual from the house of a patient, and was still engaged in my study, when my servant announced that there was a strange gentleman in the hall who was anxious to speak with me.

It was long past midnight; but a physician is bound to receive all visitors at all hours, and I bade the servant tell the stranger I would see him at once.

He entered.

It was an old man of lofty stature, but drooping carriage. The dim, uncertain light from under the shade of my lamp did not enable me to distinguish his features immediately; but he had scarcely uttered a word before I recognized Count R——.

I recognised him by his voice. In that

shadowy light I should have hardly recognised him by any other indication. It was many years since we had last met, and he was grievously altered. There are some men who preserve the aspect of youth to the extreme limit of middle age; then they seem to grow old in a year, and, as if Old Age, having finally overcome his victim, was exasperated into taking vengeance upon those features which had so long resisted his attack, these men collapse into a decrepitude which is quite disproportioned to the number of their years.

The aspect of Count Edmond R—— was like that of a broken statue. It was the painful union of beauty and ravage. His hair was still luxuriant, but snow-white. His face was ploughed with deep furrows.

There was a hopeless droop about the lines of the mouth. His gait and manner still preserved much of their old stateliness; but it was the stateliness of resignation — the dignity of a defeated man. His whole face and figure had but one expression—intense fatigue.

"If," said the Count, after we had exchanged a few commonplace salutations rendered painful by our mutual embarrassment, "if to-night I seek you once more, it is not to slip out of your hands as formerly. Shall I own to you that when we first casually encountered each other on the deck of that steamboat years (how many years?) ago, I was vexed and displeased by the pertinacious scrutiny of your regard? Accustomed, however, to let pass all such impressions without allowing them to disturb my habitual equanimity, I was surprised that I could not, in this instance, entirely rid my mind of the recollection of that passing encounter, nor shake off the peculiar, but indefinite, sensation which I first experienced on perceiving that your attention was fixed on me. It was not an agreeable sensation, nor one which I wished to prolong; and a few years afterwards, when I twice came unexpectedly and unwillingly upon you—when I twice found in you (and that, I am well assured, without any premeditation upon your part) an unsummoned witness to scenes in which you saw me under deep emotion—I began to surmise that it might possibly be something more than blind chance which thus seemed to insist on establishing relations between two persons so far removed from each other by the ordinary circumstances of life. For before we met again at the hell in the Rue ——, I had detected (though too late) your presence on a spot where I had believed myself utterly alone—by the Mare d'Auteuil. Since then, I have frequently felt myself impelled to approach you—either by the inward voice of my destiny, or perhaps only by the vulgar desire to clear up what I conceived to be an error. But ever I have hesitated and hung back rather than risk a step which might perhaps prove destructive to a certain dumb hope that has long since become a sort of consolatory custom to my thoughts, and to which I am constrained to cling with a confidence derived from despair in other sources of comfort.

"This last attempt, therefore, I have put off as long as it was in my power to do so. That it is no longer in my power to refrain from it, is proved by my presence in your house to-night."

I cannot attempt to describe to you the sort of shudder with which I listened to these words. They were uttered quite simply, and without any symptom of extraordinary emotion. But precisely on this account—precisely in proportion to the simplicity of the speech itself, and the unaffected frankness of the avowal thus made by a man whom I knew to be both sensitively proud and a consummate master in the art of repressing his emotions—I felt a sudden repugnance to receive the confession which he now seemed resolved to impose upon my confidence. Any such act of confidence upon his part had been so long withheld,—any such avowal of weakness must, I felt assured, have been wrung from such a desperate conviction of defeat,—that this consideration, added to the sense of apprehension and dismay with which I was affected by the accents of a voice which vibrated strangely under the weight of an excessive melancholy, seemed to give to the decision which I might be called upon to pronounce respecting facts yet unknown to me—a responsibility too solemn to be lightly undertaken. The moment which I had once ardently desired was come. I was afraid of it. I shrank back, and remained silent. I could not belie the gravity of my own feelings by the utterance of any commonplace assurances.

He seemed to understand this. For, as though he had not expected any reply, he continued after a momentary pause:—

"A thousand circumstances of seemingly small account," he said, "combined to urge me unceasingly upon the path which was destined to bring me here. As though half the world were in a conspiracy to bring us together, seldom a year would pass by, but what your name reached me from the most unexpected quarters, and always in some such way as seemed to place you, maugre my own disinclination, in strange and significant intercourse with my mind.

"One of those chances became at last decisive. One of those chances which must remain inexplicable if we do not regard them as whispers from that mysterious Prompter who forces us dull players to perform the parts assigned to us in the Great Tragedy of Human Life."

His voice faltered a moment, but he hastily resumed :—

"My bookseller sends me periodically the new books of the season. One day my glance fell carelessly upon the printed wrappage of one of those parcels which I had not yet opened. My attention was instantly arrested and absorbed by these words :—'*The vision exists for the actor, but for him only. It presupposes his action. The series of criminal thoughts alone, without result of any kind in action (an A without a B) cannot produce permanent or periodical appa-*

ritions. At least I know of no such case.' Perhaps you have looked deep enough into my life to divine the impression which these words made upon me. If an oracle had appeared upon the wall in characters of fire, such a miracle could not have so profoundly affected me, as this dry reflection of another human mind upon a piece of printed paper. I sent instantly for the work from which this sheet had been torn. Eagerly I turned to the title-page. The author's name was on it. The author's name was yours. Since then, your book has become the constant companion of my thoughts."

He stopped abruptly, and seemed almost overpowered. I could not answer him. With an obvious effort, he continued:—

"I will come at once to the object of my visit here to-night. That case which was wanting to your experience—"

Again he stopped, and pressed his hand to his forehead as though he felt his brow must burst with the surrender of a secret, now for the first time wrenched from the deepest roots of a life.

"That case," he repeated, "which you failed to find, I offer it to you. I would place it in your hands, for I feel my end approach. If the knowledge of evil can serve the cause of good, be it yours to dispose of. Spare me the pain of being myself your guide along that thorny path over which the bleeding traces of a tired pilgrim will suffice to point the way. These papers—take them: read them."

He rose; placed a packet of papers in my hand, and his address; bowed,—and hurriedly turned to the door.

"One question!" I exclaimed. "The Countess?"

Suddenly his whole stature rose its full height. He turned round, and stood before me erect, solemn, almost awful. He lifted his hand, and looking upwards with a strange expression on his countenance, said—"Yonder, at the right hand of her husband."

CHAPTER III.

The Secret in my hands at last.

NOTHING but my own unquiet footsteps broke the profound silence of the night. I was alone. For more than an hour I continued pacing up and down the room in strong excitement, weighing in my hand that pregnant packet which I dared not open till I had composed the trouble of those emotions to which my unexpected interview with the Count had given rise.

By degrees I grew calmer; but it was nearly morning before I sat down, with something of judicial solemnity, to open those "sessions of silent thought," from which Edmond Count R—— had invoked the verdict on his life.

Letters in various handwritings (chiefly a woman's), memoranda, pages of a journal, made up the contents of the packet which the Count had placed in my hands. I read them in the order in which I found them; but a due regard for the patience and convenience of other readers (no doubt less interested than myself) compels me to reduce the substance of these documents to a summary, reserving only the permission to extract *in extenso* some of the original papers which appear to be specially important.

CHAPTER IV.

Early Days.

THE peasant sees it, for a moment, from the river, when he floats his raft down the rapid waters of the Weidnitz. For there the river winds, and the trees are thick. The reaper sees it all day long, envying, perhaps, the shadow and the cool of it, when the sun is hot upon the red corn-lands beyond the woody upland slopes. It is an old Château that has seen many changes, and suffered few. A massive pile of grey stone, with tall copper roofs, built four-square about a quiet court. There the grass has a will of its own, and pushes its way, under trying circumstances, between the chinks in the much-flawed pavement. There, too, the sundial is always conspicuous, but the sun seldom. The south front is flanked by a square, flat garden (Italian style), with long, straight walks, whereto you descend from a broad terrace by a flight of stone stairs. The garden leads to a bowling alley. In the middle of the garden is a fish-tank, full of old red fish, and old black water. Beyond this is the park. It is not like your English parks, but rather a sort of slovenly meadow, which rambles astray in all directions, and finally loses itself in the great woodland all round. There you may hunt the roebuck, the red deer, even, and the wild boar. Such a place for shooting and for fishing never was. For about all this the river puts its arm, lovingly and quietly, like an old friend.

This is the first scene which shapes itself before my mind's eye as I read. It is the Château of L——. And here, at ease with his family, dwells Arthur Count R——; a wealthy, high-bred, honourable, kind-hearted, perhaps somewhat weak-minded nobleman. Count Arthur married late in life. It was a love marriage, however, and, what is yet more rare, a happy one. Three children were born of this marriage. Edmond, the first-born; who for some time remained the only child, for he was four years old when his brother Felix was born. To Felix succeeded, two years afterwards, a sister, Marie.

Marie was sickly from birth, and died at three years old. The more complete had been the happiness of the Countess, the more violent was her grief for the loss of her only daughter. Heaven, however, accorded her a compensation for this loss. The earliest and tenderest friend of the Countess (the companion of her childhood), had been wedded young, very young, to the spendthrift Prince C——, in Bohemia. She died in the first year of her marriage, giving birth to a daughter; and her last request to her husband was that this infant might be confided to the care of her friend, the wife of Count Arthur R——, in Silesia.

This sacrifice was not made without reluctance by the widower. But the Prince, whatever may have been his faults, had been attached to his wife, and was deeply affected by her death. He felt himself pledged to fulfil his promise to the Princess on her death-bed. Besides, how was it possible for a young man, devoted to pleasure, to look after the infant thus left on his hands? So little Juliet was conducted to L——, and henceforth became a member of the Count's family. The Prince soon forgot his double loss in a life of debauchery at Vienna. In a few years he ran through his fortune; and one morning, finding himself with empty pockets, after an enforced settlement with his creditors, he accepted active service in the Imperial army, and fell at Aspern, at the head of his regiment.

Count Arthur, as guardian of the orphan, secured to Juliet all that could be saved from the wreck of her father's fortune; and the little girl, who had no recollection of any other home, grew up at L—— with the two boys, regarded by the members of the Count's family as one of themselves, and accustomed to regard them in return with all the affection of a sister and daughter.

Juliet was a charming child, essentially loveable, because essentially loving. All the conditions of her adopted home were of a nature to develope the great feature of her character—trustfulness.

The education of Edmond had been completed at home under paternal care.

I have no personal experience of your English public schools; but I have always regarded them as the great reservoirs of the English character. What seems to me the main defect of our German system of education, is that it is too exclusively confined to intellectual development. The motive power of man does not exist in the intellectual, but in the moral, qualities. The *quantula sapientia* that governs mankind, has been a subject of continual wonder to the contemplative portion of the human community. But the explanation of this apparent phenomenon, is probably to be found in a fact too commonly ignored, and yet hardly to be disputed, viz.: that the governing qualities are moral, rather than intellectual. Our lives, and our influence upon the lives of others, are much less dependent upon intellectual superiority than is generally supposed. It is a common saying, that Knowledge is Power; but the kind of knowledge thereby implied, requires definition. Perhaps it would be more generally true, to say Power is Knowledge. It cannot in any case be asserted that book-learning is power. The chief object of education should not be the accumulation of information, but the formation of character; and I know of no system of education by which this object is so well attained as that of the English public schools.

It is not so much acuteness of the dialectic faculty, high culture, or extended range of contemplation, that governs mankind; but rather energy, sympathy, perseverance, conciliation, enthusiasm. And in all the practical affairs of life, even men of the highest intellect must probably rely rather upon the exercise of (what you would call) their second-rate, than of their first-rate, qualities. As regards the education of youth, I doubt if there can be any better principle than that embodied in the well-known maxim of the Spartan king; for, after all, it is not of the highest importance that boys should become scholars, but it *is* of the highest importance that they should become *men.* And this conviction leads me to express an opinion with regard to the theory of government as having reference to the general education of man; to which opinion I have been brought by a consideration of the principles of representative government as practised in England. It appears to me that the relative merits of representative, and arbitrary, or bureaucratic, government are generally discussed (especially on the Continent) within far too narrow a limit. The great question in which the world should be interested is not what is the completest and strongest form of a government? but what is the completest and grandest form of a people? No efficiency in the mechanism of an irresponsible government can compensate for the absence of that active power which is only to be found in the public life of a responsible people.

The clumsiest motion of a living body is preferable to the best-directed gesticulations of a galvanized corpse. The English system of government begins almost at the cradle of the Englishman; and the English system of education continues to his grave. In this, I think, exists the paramount excellence of both. In England the public school, the household, the vestry-room, the bench of magistrates, are seats of self-government; the polling-booth, the hustings, the House of Commons, the Press, the Bar, are schools for self-education. In Germany all this is wanting. Here education stops at the University, and the intellect of the nation is either absorbed into the pedantry of a bureaucracy, or remains in a state of political childhood.

But I have wandered too far from the Château at L——. I return to my wethers.

The solitude of Edmond's childhood, his education at home, the absence of companions of his own age, his premature intercourse with grown-up persons, gave to the boy's disposition, which was naturally thoughtful and reflective, a seriousness not common to his age. When the birth of his brother and sister, and a few years later, the entrance of Juliet into the family, introduced a more animated life into the old Château, Edmond, who was by some years their elder, and whose character was prematurely developed, found himself, in his relations with the other children, invested with an almost paternal character.

Thus, almost from infancy, his fraternal affection for Felix and Juliet assumed a depth of earnest tenderness, a sense of protecting duty, somewhat strange to the character of a child. There is nothing like that *camaraderie* which exists in the nursery. It shares all things together, tears and laughter, triumph and dismay, memory and hope. But when this loving, careless fellowship between companions in childhood is mingled with the sentiment of respect, it has in it an adoration and enthusiasm unequalled by anything in the more conscious relations of after life. It escapes, as it were, from the little succouring hands into the earnest eyes of childhood. How proudly they smile, those trustful eyes, upon the little hero or heroine of our first adoration! How sweet it is, in our moments of early trial, to feel the gladdening glance which assures our fluttering anxious heart that the chosen object of our emulous devotion has comprehended the struggle, and shares the triumph of some youthful effort! Schiller has beautifully indicated this sentiment in the boyish relations between Posa and Carlos.

Felix and Juliet looked up to Edmond as to a superior being His information was extraordinary in one so young. His nature was ambitious, his understanding keen, and his enthusiasm quickly excited by whatever presented itself before him in the form of a duty.

Devotedly attached to these little ones, he could not bear the thought of their education being entrusted to strange hands. And he contrived so well to convince his father of his vocation and ability to become their teacher, that the pride of the old Count was flattered by the consent which he felt himself unable to withhold from the serious charge thus enthusiastically assumed by his firstborn and favourite child. This somewhat strange position which Edmond henceforth occupied between his parents and these two children, seemed to result so naturally from the precocious maturity of his character, that it did not involve any apparent assumption on his part, nor any conscious weakness on the part of his father. He exerted no pressure upon those around him; they exerted no pressure upon him. Thus, his rarely-gifted nature harmoniously and equably developed itself without experiencing any external restraint, but also without the inward incentive of any strong passion. Felix was passionately proud of his brother. Juliet looked up to Edmond with all the romantic ardour of an enthusiastic girl. But in this life, so free from struggle and contrariety, the weapons of the will rested unused, and the vigilant eye of mistrustful Reason closed, well pleased and self-assured, upon the peace of a happy soul.

Thus the days passed by. At last the career chosen by Felix for himself rendered necessary his entry into a military school. The times were troubled; but without this circumstance, family necessities, and the disposition of the boy himself would, in any case, have decided Felix to enter the army.

This change in the customary life at L—— induced Edmond to think of completing his own education by travel and intercourse with the life of foreign countries. His first journey was to England. Early initiated, as he had been, into the business of country life and the management of a great property, this country had peculiar attractions for the young Count. His time there was not misspent. He made himself acquainted with various agricultural improvements, which he was afterwards enabled to introduce with great advantage into the cultivation of the L—— estate. But he only came into contact with that external and superficial aspect of English life which was most consonant to his own disposition, viz., that sort of methodic reticence of manner which constitutes the English notion of *Becomingness*. In England, the betrayal of emotion beyond a certain limit laid down by *commune consensus* and general authority, is, under all circumstances, *unbecoming*. Let the heart bleed, let the soul exult, let the breast feel ready to burst, when all the arms of Briareus seem insufficient to clasp to the beating heart what it yearns to embrace,—and for all this, ay, and yet more, there is, by public permission, only one set tone of voice, and only one gesture,—that invariable *shake-hands.*

It was not, therefore, by his superficial and passing intercourse with a nation which is perhaps the most earnest and impassioned in the world, that Edmond suspected even the existence of what was as yet unknown to his experience of himself,—those internal hurricanes and tornados, which sleep perhaps unroused for years in the heart of man, but which, when once let loose, are all the more violent and destructive in proportion as the will may have neglected the foundation and enlargement of those bulwarks, which are unconsciously built up by men who in early life have had to struggle with the storms of a tempestuous childhood.

Of all the wonders of London, none more fascinated the attention of the young Count than that magnificent collection of objects of interest which the English need of inquiry, seeking to satisfy itself with acquisition, not only in all ages of the past, but in all parts of the world, has amassed in the metropolis within the walls of the British Museum.

The marvels of the East were then barely opened to the curiosity of the West. And here, for the first time in his life, Edmond found himself confronted with the mystic memorials of a wonderful world long since disappeared from the face of the earth, and the unintelligible but suggestive symbols of a vast and vanished epoch of human culture. His ardent desire to visit Egypt (perhaps the cradle of all our knowledge) ripened with each visit to those treasures. He commenced with zeal the preliminary studies necessary for such an enterprise.

Subsequently he went to Paris, and visited with Champollion himself the various monuments brought there by Napoleon.

Full of impatience, he set out for Marseilles; and thence embarked for the East. Well provided with letters of credit and all necessary recommendations, he reached Cairo, that *nonchalant* sentry-box before the fairy palace of the Orient which the Turks have established on the ruins of Memphis. There he hired and equipped a boat for the journey up the Nile, engaged a dragoman recommended by the English Consul, and, taking with him his Herodotus, his

Strabo, and a firman from Constantinople, he set forth to traverse that antique road on which the human intellect has marched for a thousand centuries, and reach the immortal ruins that yet retain the world's last traces of that Pythagorean Mind which darkly, faintly, meets us in the remote and glimmering avenues of the Greek philosophy.

Various pages of the journal placed in my hands by the Count indicate the interest and ardour with which he prosecuted his Oriental researches; but the scientific journal of this expedition was not confided to me with the other papers contained in the packet. Of the events of that journey only a single episode is recorded in those papers. The results of it in the subsequent life of Count Edmond were far more important than he could possibly have anticipated when this journal was written.

CHAPTER V.

A MUMMY THAT FINDS MEANS TO MAKE ITSELF UNDERSTOOD.

IT was at Thebes.

The archæological researches of Count Edmond had brought him to that antique seat of the three last dynasties, under whose sceptre, after the expulsion of the alien conquerors, the arts and sciences of Egypt attained so vast a development, that one cannot but admire as almost miraculous the destruction by Cambyses of a fabric so colossal as that of which no more than the meagre and broken outlines are revealed in the enormous magnitude of its monumental remains.

Pitching his tent from spot to spot, now amidst the ruins of Luxor, now near the village of Carnac, Edmond could not reconcile himself to leave this land of marvel and of mystery till his imagination had exhausted every tangible material from which to reconstruct that hundred-gated wonder of the ancient world.

And thus, in the record now submitted to my inspection, of those wandering but not unlaborious days passed by the Count among the tombs, I seemed to see him,—often surprised by the great sunrise of the Orient in the prosecution of his indefatigable excavations; while the bright and dewless dawn of the Desert is enlarging its noiseless light over that vast plain which, stretched broad on either side of the Nile, unites with the Arabian range in the far east, the western summits of the Libyan hills. Or else in the wide red light of hot and windless evenings, bowed above some crumbling byblus or papyrus, in patient solitary study, a slowly-darkened figure, silent as its shadow on the sand.

On one such evening the record shows him seated upon the wall of that gigantic terrace which, although builded entirely of brick, yet stands at a height of twenty feet, and measures no less than one thousand feet in breadth and two thousand in length. On the colossal pedestal, thus formed for a fabric no less enormous, stands, with its face fronting the Nile, the Temple of Ammon Chnouphis, the Divine Originative Principle.

This immense edifice, of which the circumference extends over a space of about three English miles, is approached by an alley formed of six hundred colossal sphinges. There were within it chambers vast enough to contain the entire pile of any average-sized mediæval cathedral; and in each chamber one hundred and thirty-four enormous columns, of which only the ruins now remain, once supported a ceiling so richly decorated with painting and sculpture, that not a hand's-breadth of its spacious surface is bare of ornament.

Beyond these stupendous structures, and well worthy of a people whose enormous works were but the bodies of enormous thoughts, that famous lake, which, more than a thousand years before it was witnessed with wonder by Herodotus, had been vouchsafed by the art of man to the need of nature, still conducts to the Necropolis—a city of tombs and temples, whose streets of catacombs are hewn in the solid rock of the Libyan mountains.

Over the mysterious waters of this lake, to the neighbouring City of the Dead, had once glided (perhaps at that very hour, millions of evenings ago) the ghostlike barks that bore from the dwellings of living man the bodies of the departed. Across this lake, age after age, generations upon generations had silently sailed away from the sight of the sun. And now they were all departed. And in the place that knew them no more the only living man on whose face at that hour the sinking sunlight fell, was a wanderer from lands undreamed of by the science of those starry priests who one by one had paced along that shattered pavement, and passed along that lonesome lake, into the unseen world.

Amply furnished with an Imperial firman and all other necessary documents, Count Edmond had previously set his numerous attendants to work upon this spot; where now, completely uncompanioned, he had withdrawn himself from his retinue, in order, at his ease, and without interruption, to question the dead of secrets withheld from a thousand generations. He had just disengaged from the sheathing *byssus* in which it was preserved the mummy of a young man—perhaps a king's son.

That marvellously conservative science of the Egyptians had, in this instance, successfully disputed with time the possession of a body, whose minutest atoms had for centuries been claimed in vain by the inexorable potency of corruption. The mummy was intact, perfect, complete. Stretched supine upon the sand, beneath the close and eager countenance of the German, lay the body of the young Egyptian prince; whose life had probably not numbered more than the years of the living man now breathing over him, when from that long empty husk the breath of it had departed three thousand years ago. And, although in this parched and shrunken simulacrum of a human form the vital juices were withered up, yet the face of it retained upon its features the unchanged expression of the life which had once filled them. The hues and fulness, the bloom and substance, of this picture of man were faded and fallen away, but the hard outline of it remained distinct and undisturbed. And, as the skilful botanist instinctively recognises in the withered flower which he examines all the once flourishing beauty of it, so Edmond, from long familiarity with those dry human specimens, had by degrees acquired a certain strange faculty of mind which enabled him, if not to bring them back to life, yet to transport himself back into the life which was once theirs; and thus, by concentrating the force and intensity of a vivid imagination, to mingle, as though he were the ghost and they the real existences, amongst those generations who, in times indefinitely remote, transmitted from age to age, as we to-day transmit, as others will transmit to-morrow, the warm and beating pulse of life.

According to the custom common to the Egyptians, in respect to the arrangement of the dead, this mummy was accompanied by a papyrus; and this papyrus Edmond was now busily engaged in the attempt to decipher. Here, in the desert, where to the student of the past the somewhat artificial atmosphere of the library and the lecture-room is replaced by the animating presence of realities, and the undisturbed inspiration of Nature herself, the Count had frequently succeeded, perhaps more by intuition than research, in interpreting those hieroglyphic images which, for the most part, when found in tombs or sarcophagi, represent, with little variation, the mysterious story of the migration of the soul after death; from the moment in which she leaves the body to that in which, accompanied by the two presiding genii, she stands before the solemn Balance of the Supreme Judgment. Of this mystic balance, one scale contains the Vial of Iniquity, a vase supposed to be filled with the sins of the soul, on which judgment is about to be passed; whilst in the opposing scale is placed a feather, an image finely conceived and of singular subtlety, representing the good actions achieved by the soul in her past existence.

Although the Babylonian rite was doubtless very different from that of the Egyptians, yet in all that regards the relations of man to the unseen powers, one prevalent sentiment was so common to the various religions of Eastern antiquity,—and, even in the Hebrew theosophy, so strong a substratum of Egyptian thought is to be detected,—that any one who at this day peruses the strange pictures on these Egyptian papyri, may not unreasonably recall the appalling pages in which the Book of Daniel records the destruction of Babylon, with a strong impression that in the interpretation given to the Babylonian king by the Hebrew seer of that unknown writing on the wall, there must have been an alarming significance of something more than merely *earthly* doom; and that Belshazzar may have well turned pale when the fingers of a man's hand came forth and wrote the sentence of his proved unworth, "*Thou art weighed in the balance and found wanting.*"

Between two sphinges, the symbols of wisdom, Helios and Anubis preside at the decisive ceremonial of Divine Justice. Thoth, who is easily to be recognised by the head of the Ibis, which invariably surmounts the otherwise human figure of the god, is writing the mystic record of the Soul's Trial. Before him, Harpocrates, the god of silence, is seated (somewhat uncomfortably it would appear to any but a superhuman personage) on the upper part of the crook of a divining-wand. His finger is placed upon his lips. Finally, on his throne, before the doors of the nether world, is seated the Lord and

Master of All, the Divine Osiris, ready to deliver the final sentence on which are depending the future migration of the soul till the period of her purification, and the length and nature of her new probation.

But the particular papyrus which Edmond was now examining, differed somewhat from the majority of these passports for Eternity. On this document a long series of images preceded the description of the soul's judgment; as though it had been sought to represent certain extraordinary scenes in the previous life of the dead man.

Between the slender figures of two youths was traced the more lofty stature of a man of mature age. This central figure was represented standing upright, clothed with the insignia of royalty, and holding in the right hand, which was uplifted, a ring; with which the figure appeared to be pointing to a throne, roughly indicated by a rude outline, in the same compartment. Certain hieroglyphic characters, inscribed above the heads of the three images, seemed to indicate the names of the persons thus represented. By comparing these inscriptions with the names of the various Pharaohs of the ancient dynasties, engraved both in the hieroglyphic and the cursive character upon the numerous monuments and papyri which he had already investigated, Edmond was enabled to decipher and translate them. He could have no doubt that the central figure of the elder personage represented the last sovereign of the nineteenth dynasty, the Thoûoris of Manethon, elsewhere mentioned as Rhamses, the ninth of that name; the two other figures to the right and left, being probably (for there is no mention of them in the historic registers), Sethos and Amasis, the two sons of Thoûoris, who did not succeed to the throne.

A second series of images, placed under the first compartment, and divided from it by a border decorated by the repetition, along a horizontal riband, of the initial symbol of the human figure, represented Amasis, the younger of the two princes, inscribing various characters upon a papyrus; whilst, at the same time, he holds, uplifted in the left hand, a ring, which is no doubt the same as that which, in the first compartment, appears in the right hand of the king. In this picture Amasis appears to be translating and inscribing on the papyrus certain characters engraved upon the amulet of the ring. Sethos, the elder brother, with his back turned to the throne, is represented in the act of walking away.

The third picture, divided in the same manner from the second, shows the two brothers, each in a boat by himself, rowing upon a stream which is doubtless that of the Nile.

In the fourth and last group of historic figures, Sethos is alone upon the water. He is standing at the prow of his boat, with folded arms. The other boat is upset, and a wave of the river is indicated as passing over it. Amasis has disappeared. Only an arm and hand, which is probably that of the drowning prince, is stretched above the surface of the water. And on the finger of that outstretched hand appears the ring which has already figured with such apparent significance in the three preceding pictures.

From this point commences the series of images which represents the migration of the soul of Amasis. The soul rises from the heart of the dead in the shape of a bird,* bearing in her beak the sacred key of the religious mysteries. Arrived at the place of Supreme Justice, she is presented to the tribunal by the two plumed genii of the dead. Anubis, the messenger of the gods, who is represented with the head of a jackal, places beside the mystic feather,

---

* This bird is a species of falcon, named in the Egyptian *Baith*, and in other Oriental languages *Baz*. It is noteworthy that to this day the German word for a hawking-expedition is *Beize*.

in the scale of the soul's good actions, the ring, to which such frequent allusion occurs in the four historic records, immediately preceding this scene. Thus extraordinarily weighted, that scale of the mystic balance which contains the feather appears to be sinking lower than the other which contains the vial of iniquity; as though to indicate the favourable judgment of the tribunal on behalf of the soul of Amasis.*

---

* Nothing in these papyri, representing "the Judgment after Death," is more remarkable than the frequent indication of a desire on the part of the presiding Powers to adjust the balance in favour of the good actions of the soul by some extraordinary interference. This very significantly indicates the Oriental conviction of the difficulty of reconciling, without supernatural intervention in favour of man, the aggregate short-comings of human actions with the inexorable requirements of Supreme Justice. The conviction thus expressed, which predominates the

The more than ordinary interest with which Edmond now perused the mystic annals of this somewhat perplexing papyrus was augmented by the fact that the mummy itself actually carried on the forefinger of the right hand a ring containing an amethyst of extraordinary size and beauty, on which were engraved precisely the same characters as those which Thoth was represented in the papyrus as inscribing on the records of the soul's judgment.

So profoundly was he absorbed in the

---

whole of the Hebrew Scriptures from Moses to the Prophets, has no less deeply entered into the dogma of modern Christianity, which asks in fear and trembling, "Who then can be saved?" "Use every man after his deserts," says Hamlet, "and who shall 'scape whipping?"

minute examination of these strange and unintelligible images, that he had been utterly unconscious of the noiseless approach of a man, who, now standing beside him, with arms folded on his breast, in an attitude of intense and melancholy attention, had been for some moments past the tacit witness of the Count's occupations. Nor was it, indeed, till the sun, now low on the western horizon, had in its silent and stealthy prolongation of the shadows of all things, cast over the record he was perusing the dark adumbration of the stranger's tall and stately figure, that his attention was attracted towards the cause of that silent but sudden interruption.

Edmond uplifted his eyes with an amazement which was certainly not diminished by anything in the character of the apparition upon which they rested. Draped in the massive folds of that flowing milk-white vesture which gives to its dusky wearers a dignity of form so statuesque, that in their moments of motionless repose they look like antique images of mingled marble and bronze, there stood, dark-eyed, dark-visaged, and gazing down intensely into the startled face of the young German, one of those Kabyl chieftains whose daring raids for plunder are the terror of the travellers of the Desert.

So majestic in its immoveable serenity, yet marked withal by such severity of strength in the supple grace of its sinewy stature, so suggestive of powers hostile to man, did that solitary image appear, as it stood darkly and keenly outlined against the lurid levels of the glaring west, that it might almost seem as though the silence and the solitude of the desert had suddenly heaped themselves into palpable form, and there stood in stern and sinister contemplation of their invader.

The first impulse of the Count was one of self-defence. His hand made a rapid and involuntary movement towards the double-barrelled rifle which was lying on the sand beside him. The Arab, without any change of attitude or gesture, replied to this avowal of suspicion and alarm only by a look of that inimitable contempt which is never attained but by the features of the Orientals; and in which, whenever we Europeans are forced to encounter it, we are conscious of the supreme condemnation of our habitual self-satisfaction. It is a rebuke to which there is no reply; a sentence from which there is no appeal. It was not without a blush, of which he was painfully conscious, that Edmond lowered his eyes abashed from that look of tranquil scorn on the face of the Kabyl chief.

An instant's reflection sufficed to convince him of the ridiculous and humiliating inutility of any attempt at self-defence; for it was sufficiently obvious that, had any attack been intended, it might long since have been made with the certainty of success.

"Disturb not, stranger, the repose of the tomb. It is not well for the living to hold parley with the dead."

It was a warning, rather than a reproach

or a menace, which Edmond felt to be conveyed to him by these words, abruptly uttered in that *Lingua Franca* which, throughout the Orient, forms a neutral ground of language whereon the various races of the East and West may encounter each other upon equal terms.

Pleased with any pretext for escape from his previous embarrassment, and well content to find one in the common resources of conversation, the Count hastened to reply to this sudden appeal.

"You might say well," he answered, "if this tomb were less taciturn than I have found it. It obstinately refuses, however, to answer my question. And yet I have not sought from it any secret of the other world. I simply ask it to restore to this life what from this life it has robbed."

"Fool!" said the Arab; "and who hath told thee it is good for the living that the tomb should restore to their knowledge the secrets it is bidden to withhold? Knowest thou aught of the nature of any force, and whether it be of good or of evil, so long as that force is hidden, and the action of it laid to sleep?"

"Certainly," murmured Edmond, half to himself, "I know not of any force of which I can conceive that it should retain the faculties of action after a slumber so immeasurably prolonged."

The stranger did not immediately reply. A profound melancholy seemed to darken in the intricate depths of the luminous eye which he fixed upon the Count, as he slowly answered, after a momentary silence:—

"Say you so? Yet a grain of corn, taken from the tomb to-day, and cast into the furrow to-morrow, will grow from the blade cut down by the sickle that reaped in the harvests of the Pharaohs, ere the glory of these was gathered into the garners of Time. And can you doubt of the immortality of forces far mightier than those that germinate in the grain of corn which you take from the tomb where they slumber; or suppose that the centuries, survived by the seed of the field, can annihilate the seed of the soul?"

Edmond was no less struck by the peculiar tone of voice with which these words were uttered than by the accuracy of the illustration they suggested; for he had frequently convinced himself of the fact that corn found deposited with mummies in symbol of sacrifice, perfectly retains its faculty of germination.

"After all, though," he replied, "if I must grant you the existence of the fact to which you allude, yet I confess that I can think of nothing except a blade of corn from which this sort of palingenesis can be expected."

The Arab approached the mummy that was lying on the sand before the Count. He stood over the wizened corpse for some time in profound silence. The ardent and intense regard of those dark and intricate eyes was plunged in piercing scrutiny upon the withered features of the dead man's brown, adust, and stolid face. Not a muscle was moved on the cheek of the Kabyl. Under the lustrous transparency peculiar to the complexion of Orientals, nothing agitated the stern metallic reflection of the firm bronzen features, not less brown nor less immoveable than those of the mummy at his feet. But ever and anon from beneath the mysterious languors and soft depth of shadow with which the long, slumbrous eye-lash veiled the vigilant eye, Edmond could notice, not without an emotion far from comfortable, that strange lights and flashes, as though struck out from some fierce agony of soul, were passing and darting in lurid, sinister play.

Suddenly at length the Arab stretched

forth his swarthy arm, and seized the dead man's hand. He drew the ring from its withered finger, and fixed his glittering eye upon the purple, luminous stone, intently perusing the characters engraved upon it.

"Yes," he muttered, as though continuing aloud some dialogue commenced within himself, — "Behold the fateful words of Seb Kronos, the Indestructible Destroyer! .... MINE IS THE WORLD, AND TO ME MUST ALL THINGS COME. I, SOLE, HAVE CREATED; AND I, SOLE, DESTROY. I WILL WHAT I WILL. I GIVE AND I TAKE AWAY. ON MORTALS I BESTOW, AND FROM MORTALS I WITHHOLD, HAPPINESS. MAN, THAT ART MADE OF THE DUST OF THE EARTH, DISTURB NOT THE HAND OF DESTINY. TOUCH NOT WITH EARTHLY FINGER THE WORK OF FATE."

"Tell me," exclaimed Edmond; "is that indeed the sense of the amulet?"

"It is the *words* of the amulet," said the other, and he passed the ring into the hand of the Count. "Blessed thou," he added, after a pause, "if thou never ascertain the sense of them. He that first discovered the significance of those words lies stretched before thee. Behold the first victim of the oracle!"

The Arab pointed to the mummy at his feet. Then taking the papyrus from the hand of Edmond: "Lo, here," he said, "Thoûoris and his sons; Sethos the elder, Amasis the younger.

"Ignoring the prerogative of birthright, the king areads the monarchy to him that shall read the riddle of the ring, as being the most wise and worthiest to reign. Verily not wise was he that thus reversed the rule of Nature. Now, of the sons of Thoûoris, the most wise was Amasis. Forasmuch as in him was an excellent spirit of knowledge, to understand the writings of the gods, and in the showing forth of hard sentences. He, therefore, to his hurt, resolved the riddle of the ring.

"DISTURB NOT THE HAND OF DESTINY.

"TOUCH NOT WITH EARTHLY FINGER THE WORK OF FATE.

"So Amasis read the writing, and declared the interpretation thereof. Deeply within his inmost heart, Sethos kept those words. Even as they were graven upon the stone of the ring, so also were they graven upon the spirit of the man.

"And from him the Most High God removed the kingdom and the glory of it: so that the sceptre departed out of the hand of Sethos and was given to his brother, that he should sit on the throne of his fathers after the death of Thoûoris the king.

"Then Sethos bowed his head, and was obedient to the will of the Most High God, revering the words of the Oracle.

"But neither did he forget those words in the after time. Therefore, he lifted not his hand, neither in anywise hindered he the work of the Inevitable, when to him his brother (was it not by the fault of the man himself? and was it not by the will of the Most High?) being in evil case, a drowning man and without help, stretched forth from out of the whelming of the waters, a suppliant hand.

"And so Amasis perished under the eye of his brother Sethos. For the waters took him, and he died."

"And what became of Sethos?" exclaimed Edmond, whose imagination was stretched to the utmost by the strange recital which thus suddenly illuminated the hitherto unelucidated obscurity of that antique tragedy imaged on the papyrus which he had in vain been attempting to decipher.

A bitter smile played about the hard-lined angles of the lips of the Kabyl chief.

"Saidest thou not thyself," he answered (and a look of inexpressible mockery accompanied these words, slowly and emphatically pronounced), "Saidest thou not thyself that thou seekest not from the tomb the secrets of another world?"

Edmond, again overmastered by the supreme mockery which he felt in the tone of this response, was compelled to lower his eyes from the face of the Kabyl. They rested on the gem which he yet held in his hand. The mystic amethyst seemed to dart at him from the glittering and vindictive angles of its luminous facets violet forked fires, and flashes of unholy light.

Meanwhile the sun had sunk unnoticed behind the dark summits of the Libyan mountains. And now the large disc of the full moon was swathing in soft, argent light the hot, transparent air, and sultry spaces of the great solitude. When the Count again lifted up his eyes, he perceived that the mysterious inhabitant of that solitude had left his side as noiselessly as he had approached it. He could indistinctly trace the tall form of the Desert's dusky son, silently gliding into darkness among the mighty trunks of the colossal columns of the temple of Ammon Chnouphis.

END OF VOL. I.